THE HEART SURGEON'S SECRET CHILD

BY

MEREDITH WEBBER

MILLS & BOON®
Pure reading pleasure™

First published in Great Britain 2008
Paperback edition 2009
Harlequin Mills & Boon Limited,
Eton House, 18-24 Paradise Road, Richmond, Surrey TW9 1SR

© Meredith Webber 2008

ISBN: 978 0 263 86818 0

Set in Times Roman 10½ on 12¾ pt
03-0109-51215

Printed and bound in Spain
by Litografia Rosés, S.A., Barcelona

Meredith Webber says of herself, 'Some ten years ago, I read an article which suggested that Mills and Boon were looking for new medical authors. I had one of those "I can do that" moments, and gave it a try. What began as a challenge has become an obsession— though I do temper the "butt on seat" career of writing with dirty but healthy outdoor pursuits, fossicking through the Australian Outback in search of gold or opals. Having had some success in all of these endeavours, I now consider I've found the perfect lifestyle.'

Recent titles by the same author:

CHILDREN'S DOCTOR, MEANT-TO-BE WIFE†
THE SHEIKH SURGEON'S BABY*
DESERT DOCTOR, SECRET SHEIKH*
A PREGNANT NURSE'S CHRISTMAS WISH
THE NURSE HE'S BEEN WAITING FOR†

*Desert Doctors
†Crocodile Creek

PROLOGUE

'IT's a love letter, you can't deny that!'

The tall, slim young woman stood in front of him, anger sparking from her greeny-brown eyes, hurt and defiance yelling at him from the taut white face and tense lines of her body. 'You've a wife at home, and you've betrayed her with me! Men!'

'But it was over with. There—'

She didn't let him finish, turning away to lift one, then two, then three babies into her arms, while outside the orphanage an even wilder storm raged, nature gone berserk.

'Not as far as she was concerned, that's obvious from an envelope festooned with pink hearts,' Lauren snapped. 'Not to mention *"Je t'aime"* which even an Aussie idiot can recognise as French for I love you. And the name— Therese Fournier—I doubt she's your sister!'

She stood there, clasping the babies, her body vibrating with her rage. Jean-Luc wrapped a threadbare blanket around her shoulders then around the babies. It would offer poor protection from the slashing rain that fell outside but he had to try. He had to try to calm her, too, to explain, although he knew he'd failed, her rejection obvious as she shrugged off the fingers he let linger on her arm.

'I should have known,' she continued, anger still reverberating from every cell as she walked swiftly towards the door, body bent above the precious bundles in her arms. 'Should have known a man as good-looking and sophisticated and worldly as you are wouldn't really have been interested in a naïve little idiot like me! Except for sex, of course!'

'It wasn't like that but this isn't the time—' Jean-Luc began, but Lauren was too wound up—too wounded—to listen to anything he had to say.

'Of course it's the time,' she retorted, as quick as a pistol shot. 'There's a typhoon raging out there, and we're all about to be swept away. If we can't tell the truth now, when can we? Now, open the door so I can get these little ones over to the church. It's bad enough they have to hear the storm without them hearing us argue as well, poor wee darlings.'

He opened the door, dodging so the force of the wind behind it didn't knock him over, then he put his arms around Lauren and the babies and they pushed into the wind, dodging as flying debris came close, needing the strength of their combined efforts to get them across the twenty yards separating the orphanage and the church.

Once inside, Lauren threw off the sodden blanket and took her damp charges up towards the altar beneath which she and Jean-Luc had already nestled five other infants and laid in a supply of water, powdered milk, feeding bottles and dry biscuits. Father Joe had suggested they put the babies beneath the altar, thinking the tiny church building, built of brick, was more likely to stand against the typhoon's force than the larger but less well-built orphanage building. The only trouble was the church was little more than a chapel, too small for the older children and staff to cram into, so he, Jean-Luc and the nuns had built a kind of fortress within the orphanage, using beds and tables for walls and mattresses for a ceiling. There they intended to huddle until the typhoon passed over them and the wild winds and seas diminished.

'Lauren—' Jean-Luc began, hating to leave her alone with the babies but especially hating to leave her like this— angry and hurt.

'Go, Jean-Luc, the others need you.'

'But…'

She looked at him across the stone altar, babies cradled in her arms and such sadness in her face he thought his heart would break.

'It's as much my fault as yours,' she said bitterly. 'I loved you, so I trusted you. I believed you when you said you loved me. Look at you—how could I not love you, and, loving you, how could I not believe? Put it down to my stupidity! Now, go!'

She disappeared from view, kneeling down to put her babies with the others, to lift and soothe one already there, crying softly, as all the babies did from time to time.

Indecision held him—he wanted so much to stay, to explain he and Therese had been separated for months, *and* to offer whatever protection he might to this woman with whom, against all the odds, he'd fallen in love—but the nuns were old and frail and Father Joe needed him to help with the older children. If he hesitated a moment longer, getting back to the orphanage building might be impossible.

'We'll talk later,' he said desperately, torn in two by having to leave her but hurrying anyway towards the door.

'Oh, no, we won't.'

The words came from beneath the altar, ominous words, cold and angry, although he had no idea how prophetic they would be. Three days later, lying in hospital with a shattered leg, and less serious injuries too numerous to list, he recalled how, only two hours after he'd left Lauren and the babies in the church, the freak wave that had washed away the orphanage and carried him up into the foothills beyond the village had also reduced the church to a pile of bricks and rubble.

Lauren was dead…

CHAPTER ONE

JEAN-LUC sniffed the air as he walked the short distance from the hospital to his temporary home. The huge park that stretched out on the opposite side of the road made it hard to believe he was in a big city. Not that he'd seen much of it, apart from this small corner, but flying in he'd seen the harbour and the fabled Opera House, and he knew the beach-side suburbs of Bondi and Coogee—such strange names—were not far away.

Sydney! Ten years ago he'd listened to a twenty-one-year-old young woman talk with rapture and enthusiasm of the place that was her home, the memory returning when he'd had to choose between this city and Cincinnati, both places offering a chance to work with a first-class paediatric cardiac surgical team.

Now Lauren, with whom he'd fallen so unexpectedly in love back then, walked beside him like a ghost—perhaps a ghost that had lingered in his mind for far too long, affecting his relationships with other women…

Zut! How had such sentimental thoughts crept into his mind? The long flight must have left him more tired than he'd realised, to be thinking such nonsense. His engagement had ended because Justine couldn't handle his devotion to his work and his marriage to Therese had broken up long before he'd gone to India.

And Sydney had been the obvious choice because he'd met Alex Attwood at a conference and been impressed by the man. Working on his team would be enjoyable as well as a privilege.

He shoved the transient memory of Lauren back where it belonged—into the past. This was now, and his first day in the unit had been fascinating, although he'd have to start taking notes if he was to remember all the new ideas and subtle innovations he wanted to take back with him to Marseilles.

Work. It had been his focus as he'd recovered from his injuries ten years ago—indeed, with Lauren dead and his leg shattered it had been a reason to keep on living—and since then it had brought its own rewards, especially now with the offer to head up his own paediatric cardiac surgery unit at the new hospital in Marseilles!

He sniffed the air again, thinking of Marseilles and his home village of Cassis nearby—wanting to smell the sea this time—but he must be too far from those beaches.

And getting soft in the head to be thinking of such things!

'Aagh!'

The shrill cry drew him out of his imaginings and he looked around. Ahead of him a small school bus was receding into the distance and on the footpath opposite a youth was flying along on a skateboard.

Had he called out?

The cry had turned to a wail of distress and as Jean-Luc crossed the road, certain that's where the noise had origi-nated, he saw the small child lying in a crumpled heap, wailing piteously.

It wasn't hard to put the accident together—the school bus, the youth on the skateboard, getting away as fast as he could, no thought at all for his small victim. Jean-Luc reached the child and knelt beside him.

'I'm a doctor,' he said gently, removing a floppy-brimmed hat so he could see the child. 'Can you tell me where it hurts?'

The small head turned and Jean-Luc recognised the epicanthic eyelid folds of Down's Syndrome. Anger at the youth who'd knocked the little fellow over heated Jean-Luc's blood, but right now he needed to check the little boy.

'Did he run over you or just knock you down?' he asked, while dark blue eyes continued to stare at him. 'Does your head hurt?'

A nod, which could be answering anything—Jean-Luc realised he'd asked too many questions. The little boy straightened to a sitting position and brushed the back of his hand across his face to clear the tears that streaked his cheeks.

'I got a fright,' he said. 'And hurt my hand.'

He held out his hand for inspection and, sure enough, the fall had grazed it, blood welling amidst the dirty scratches. He'd grazed his left knee and leg as well but possibly those injuries weren't hurting as much as the hand and the child hadn't noticed.

Jean-Luc looked around. Surely if the bus had dropped the little boy off, someone would be waiting for him, but all the houses showed blank faces to the street, no anxious mother peering out a window or a door.

What was wrong with people that they let a vulnerable child like this out on his own?

'Do you live near here?' he asked, as his patient sniffed and dragged his schoolbag onto his lap.

A nod, then the uninjured hand lifted and a finger pointed to the house outside which they squatted.

'Number thirty,' the boy said proudly. 'Number thirty, Kensington Terrace.'

He had reason to be proud, Jean-Luc thought. For so young a child with developmental difficulties, knowing his address was a remarkable achievement.

'What if I carry you inside?' Jean-Luc suggested. 'Will your mother be at home?'

The boy nodded. 'Mum or Gran or Bill or Russ, someone's always at home.'

Then why aren't they looking out for you? Jean-Luc wondered, thinking Mum and Gran and Bill and Russ must all be remarkably laid-back or plain careless that they hadn't been watching for the bus. People these days were just too casual about the safety of their children!

He lifted the child easily, and had just stood up when a frantic barking began across the road, then the blast of a car horn, a squeal of brakes, a desperate cry of 'Lucy!' and a golden Labrador landed on the footpath right in front of them, teeth bared as he greeted Jean-Luc with a deep-throated growl.

Put that child down!

The command was implicit in the threatening noise while the child's delighted 'Lucy!' confirmed the dog was indeed the child's pet.

Before Jean-Luc could decide on his next move—would the dog bite if he moved?—a long-legged woman came racing across the road, once again causing car horns to blare and brakes to squeal. Long, dark, red-brown hair flew behind her, flopping against her head as she slid to a halt in front of Jean-Luc, green-brown eyes flashing fire.

'Put him down! How dare you? Who are you, touching my child like that?'

The dog, perhaps taking the woman's demands as permission to get more involved, began to dance around Jean-Luc, barking furiously, the entire situation developing into something very like a farce.

Except that comedy was the last thing in Jean-Luc's mind as he stared at the woman who reached out for the child, now wriggling in Jean-Luc's absent-minded grasp.

It *couldn't* be!

His mind was playing tricks.

It was because he'd been thinking of her.

'He's a doctor, Mum,' the little boy said. 'A big boy knocked me down!'

'Lucy, sit!' the woman commanded, then she snatched her child from Jean-Luc's arms.

The dog sat, but kept his dark brown eyes fixed firmly on Jean-Luc. *One false move and your hand is mine!*

'Oh, Joe, are you hurt? What big boy? Was it someone we know? Didn't the bus driver see?'

She was too busy searching her son's body for injury to notice Jean-Luc, which was perhaps just as well, for he was staring at her, dumbstruck, certain he was seeing a ghost returned to life.

That it *was* Lauren he had no doubt—the voice, slightly husky as if she always had a cold, the face, the freckles, the long, long legs—but for some strange reason the coincidence of running into her like this was not nearly as hard to believe as the fact that she was alive.

That was the miracle!

'Oh, you've hurt your hand—but everything else? You're all right?'

The little boy assured her he was OK and she hugged him to her body, finally acknowledging the presence of another person and looking across the child at Jean-Luc.

'I'm sorry,' she said, offering an apologetic smile to underline the words. 'I overreacted. Thank you for coming to the rescue. The bus must have been early. Lucy and I were just coming back from our walk. Did you see what happened? See who knocked him over?'

Jean-Luc stared at her, unable to believe she could be so oblivious. It was unthinkable that she had no idea who he was! That he could have changed so much, or been so forgettable…

'You don't remember me?'

She frowned, her lovely hazel eyes now studying him more intently, although he guessed most of her attention was still on her child and she was anxious to get him inside so she could check for herself that he wasn't seriously injured.

'Should I know you?' she asked, her smile now polite, but very distant. 'Oh, Joe said you're a doctor. You work at the hospital. Of course!' Another smile, more polite than the first and with as little meaning. 'You must forgive me. I had an accident years ago and it affected my memory, especially my memory for faces.'

A third smile, this one genuine enough to spark lights in the eyes that had once shone with love for him.

'At least, that's my excuse.' She held out her hand. 'I'm Lauren Henderson and this is Joe. Thank you once again.'

Jean-Luc took her hand and introduced himself, eyeing her carefully, certain he'd see a spark of recognition and probably embarrassment when he said his name, but far from uttering a delighted cry of 'Jean-Luc' and exclaiming over wonderful twists of fate, all she did was shake his hand and release it, her fingers dropping his so abruptly he knew her thoughts were back on the little boy.

He should have said more—reminded her of India—but she was so totally oblivious and the little boy was claiming pain in his injured hand. So Jean-Luc settled for saying goodbye and watched her scurry back towards the house, head bent as she spoke quietly to her child, the dog they'd called Lucy—surely a female name and it was definitely a male dog—following close behind them, though turning from time to time to check Jean-Luc posed no further danger. The front door opened and all three disappeared inside, the door closing behind them.

Maybe she *was* a ghost—the whole episode a figment of his imagination, brought about because he'd been thinking about Lauren and her description of her home town…

Had she met that man before? Surely not, for how could she have forgotten someone so mesmeric? Tall, dark and handsome he most certainly was, with eyes—were they dark blue or black?—deepset under black brows. Black hair, neatly trimmed, greying slightly at the temples—a cliché surely! Maybe he dyed it grey to look distinguished. If so, he'd certainly achieved his aim! Tanned olive skin, slightly scarred, puckered even in places, stretched across a strongly boned face, while a long straight nose drew the eyes to well-shaped lips.

Kissable lips!

Lauren set Joe down on the kitchen table the better to examine his injuries. Kissable lips indeed! What was she thinking?

And why?

Because her body had responded to the touch of his

hand? Because her skin had tingled when he'd clasped her fingers?

Of course not! She'd been strung up over seeing Joe in a stranger's arms—then to hear he'd been injured…

The tingling had been apprehension…

It had only happened when he'd touched her.

She used a clean cloth to wipe the grazes on Joe's hand and leg, chatting to him, asking about the accident, although her mind was not on Joe's explanations of the skateboard rider crashing into him but on the man who had rescued her son.

A stranger.

Just an ordinary man.

No! Not in the wildest flights of any woman's imagination could that man be classed as ordinary.

Or forgettable—yet she certainly had no recollection of ever having met him.

'Did he say he was a doctor?' Lauren asked, pushing her memory to bring up some hint of a meeting.

'Who?'

'The man who picked you up.'

'Yes.'

Big help!

'At the hospital?'

'Dunno. Mum, can I go and play?'

'A snack first,' Lauren said. What was she doing, cross-examining her own child about a man she'd probably never see again? She lifted Joe off the table and sent him to wash his hands.

Although the man *had* been walking down the road…

And most of the houses in the area were hospital houses…

She shook her head at her own stupidity. As if a man like

that would ever look at someone like her, and then there was her track record with men. Most men who took her out were interested right up until the stage they met Joe and realised he was part of the package, after which they disappeared, never to be heard from again.

She put a glass of milk and a plate of cheese with fruit and vegetable sticks on the table, and settled Joe in front of them. Then she ruffled his hair and bent to kiss the top of his head.

She'd rather have Joe than a thousand handsome men, although now and then she wondered wistfully about his father. Had *his* touch made her skin tingle?

The next morning Jean-Luc stood at the bedroom window of the flat that would be his home for the next six months. It was two doors down from the one where the ghost of Lauren lived—except she wasn't a ghost, she was real. Even her name, Lauren Henderson, was real.

It was unbelievable—first that she was alive, and then the coincidence of running into her, although Lauren had been set on a medical career and from what he'd been told most of the houses in the area were home to medical personnel from St James's Hospital. Jimmie's, the staff all called it—

Not what he should be thinking about—nicknames for hospitals. What he had to consider was why he was even thinking about her. So she was alive! She had obviously survived the typhoon though how, when he'd seen photos of the collapsed church and couldn't imagine anyone surviving beneath the rubble, he didn't know.

Was that the accident she'd spoken of? Was the memory loss amnesia?

Which brought him neatly back to the fact that it

didn't matter. So, an old girlfriend was living two doors away—so what?

It certainly wasn't important as far as Lauren was concerned, for she didn't have a clue who he was.

And there was no reason why things couldn't stay that way.

Except that he'd spent the night tossing and turning in his bed, fragments of their time together returning to haunt his dreams, images of how she looked now intruding into his sleep, which was extremely aggravating.

And her not remembering him made him feel…not angry but definitely put out.

'Are you coming?'

The old house in which he was living was hospital property, available for rent by visiting specialists. It was divided into two flats, and Grace Sutherland, the second of the surgical fellows working with Alex Attwood's team this term, was occupying the other one. She was tapping at his door, as she did most mornings, so they could walk to work together.

Grace chattered as they walked, talking about Theo, the Greek perfusionist on the surgical team. Was Grace really interested in the mechanics of, and possibilities of improvement to, the heart bypass machine or was her interest more personal? Jean-Luc and Grace had been in Australia less than a week, and had only met the members of the surgical team a couple of days earlier—could she be interested in a man so quickly?

Women—he would never understand them, and now he no longer tried. He'd already chalked up one failed marriage, and since the end of his engagement to

Justine—she'd accused him, perhaps justly, of being more interested in work than he was in her—he had found there were plenty of women who didn't want to be understood any more than they wanted permanence, women happy to enjoy an affair with no strings attached on either side.

And if, at times, he felt an emptiness in his life, he knew he had only to return to work—to see the babies and children he treated—and he would feel fulfilled and whole again. There was something in their innocence and trust that allowed him to forget about his relationship failures— forget even his cynicism about life in general. Being with his small patients renewed his determination to provide them all with the best possible chance at life.

'Just being with these children brings me indescribable joy,' Lauren had once said, talking of the children in the orphanage, and in his head he had often echoed those words, thinking her long gone yet finding comfort and confirmation in them.

Except she wasn't long gone—wasn't dead at all.

He strode out along the footpath, aware his steps must have slowed as he thought about Lauren, so he was trailing behind Grace who moved with athletic ease.

'Did you leave a beautiful woman behind in France? Is that why you're dreaming your way up the road?' Grace asked, stopping at the lights to wait for him to catch up.

'No beautiful woman left behind,' he told her. 'No non- beautiful woman either, except, of course, my mother and my grandmother, a brace of aunts and a horde of female cousins.'

Grace studied him.

'You're far too good-looking not to have women falling over themselves to be with you, so what's the story?'

He had to smile. His new colleague didn't know the meaning of subtle—all her questions and observations were equally blunt and often intrusive.

'Maybe I'm not interested in women,' he said, hoping to stop her probing, but she greeted this remark with a laugh, then took his arm to cross the road, the lights now showing green and a crowd hustling all around them.

'The consulting rooms and team-meeting rooms are above the theatre and PICU,' Grace reminded him as they went into the big building.

'I remember, but I'll stop on the floor below and check the babies before I go up,' he said. 'I've plenty of time.'

Grace seemed surprised, but checking the babies in his care was always the first thing he did when he entered a hospital. It was more than a habit, because even when he didn't need to see them to boost his spirits, he felt it centred him—concentrated his mind on his work, and most of all reminded him why he did what he did. So the tiny scraps of humanity on whom they operated would have a chance to live normal, useful, happy lives.

'You do your thing with the babies and I'll go on ahead,' Grace told him, her tone of voice and the look she gave him suggesting she was humouring him in some way.

Well, Grace could think what she liked. He was going to visit the babies!

Jean-Luc found his way into the PICU, where he spoke to the sister watching the monitor and learned that all the babies in the unit were stable, some doing better than others, but all progressing. He visited each one of them, learning names—Mollie, Jake, Tom—finding himself translating them into the French equivalents because that made them more personal to him. He talked to parents sitting by the cribs, introducing himself to those he hadn't met before, assuring and reassuring them.

But always the focus of his attention was the infants, most of whom slept peacefully or watched him pass with wide-open eyes.

He was leaving one of the single rooms after a quiet chat with the parents of a three-year-old recovering from a septal defect repair when a voice, so familiar he shivered at hearing it, penetrated his consciousness.

Movement on the far side of the bigger room attracted his attention and he watched as a tall woman in the smock and headscarf of a nurse led a distressed couple out of a door.

They disappeared from view but now they were outside the room he could hear their voices more clearly.

'But he's so tiny, how can he survive?' a woman wailed.

'Because he's had the best team in Australia operating on him,' came the confident answer. 'Yes, it was a traumatic operation for such a tiny baby but, believe me, the men and women in that theatre know their jobs. If anyone can sort out the problems your Jake had with his heart, that lot could. Now all we have to do is get him better.'

Impossible! Coincidence couldn't stretch that far. Although his mother always said things happened in threes and here was Lauren alive, number one, then living all but next door, number two, now working in the same unit, number three.

Impossible!

Yet this third coincidence—or twist of fate—had shaken him and he went into the small tearoom and sat down for a moment. Could he work with Lauren and not tell her of their shared past?

All their shared past?

She had a child and presumably a husband although she was still using her maiden name.

Lauren married?

It shouldn't hurt—it had been ten years…

And if she'd forgotten him, then surely that was that. No need to tell her, to remind her.

The idea made him feel extremely uneasy, and digging deep into his confused mind he decided it was pique. He felt upset that she'd forgotten him—betrayed…

Lauren led Brian and Shelley Appleton out of the PICU and into a small quiet room, one of several set aside for parents. She offered them tea or coffee but Brian was too uptight to do more than wave away the offer with his hand, pacing back and forth in the small space between the four comfortable chairs and the coffee-table.

Lauren knew she had to try again to calm the man.

'There's no guarantee he'll need another operation,' she said quietly. 'You've been reading up on it and know that in some cases children with coarctation of the aorta do need further surgery as they grow, but it doesn't happen in all cases. The surgeons have removed the narrow part of Jake's aorta that was causing him problems and rejoined the blood vessel without any difficulty or the need for a man-made tube so the outlook for him is really good.'

She looked hopefully at Brian, and knew immediately he hadn't been mollified. Though Shelley had sunk down into one of the armchairs and closed her eyes, as if removing herself from the discussion.

'Except that he'll have to keep seeing specialists, and he could get endocarditis or even golden staph.'

'Brian!'

Shelley's voice held appeal, but beyond that was exhaustion. Lauren shifted her attention.

'Can I get something for you, Shelley? A cup of something or a cold drink, a sandwich?'

'We've been living on sandwiches for the last month!' Brian stormed. 'What makes you think we'd want more of them?'

Lauren swallowed a sigh. Baby Jake had been in hospital since his birth a month earlier—of course his parents would be sick of sandwiches. But Shelley obviously needed food, and probably a change of scenery.

'Look,' Lauren said, touching Brian's arm to make him stop pacing and look at her. 'I know you're upset, and you've reason to be, but you're being too negative about this. You're also both exhausted, mentally and physically. Why don't you get out of this place for a while? Go for a walk in the park. Stop in the shade for a hug and a kiss. There's a terrific Italian restaurant on the other side of the park—get some breakfast there and a cup of real coffee, breathe fresh air, and be thankful young Jake was born in a hospital where there are facilities to treat his condition, and extra thankful he's got through the operation so well. I've spent the last three years in this kind of unit and I've never seen a baby come through an op like his as well as he did. So go somewhere and think about yourselves for a change. Think about each other, talk to each other—about yourselves not Jake.'

Brian stared at her and Lauren wondered if he'd heard a word she'd said, then he grinned, looking about ten years younger, more like his real age, which she knew was thirty.

'A hug and a kiss sounds OK,' he said, then he turned to his wife. 'Shell?'

Shelley smiled, though tiredly, and looked at Lauren, who nodded firmly, mouthing, 'Go.'

'OK, we'll take a walk.'

Shelley stood up and linked her arm through her husband's.

'But I'm not making any promises about hugs or kisses,' she added, a real smile this time taking years off her face, too. 'You'll look after Jake?'

'As if he were my own,' Lauren promised, not bothering to add she should have finished her night shift several hours ago. These people had needed her, and though Jake didn't—he'd have extremely competent nurses watching him—she'd stay, because she'd said she would.

She watched the Appletons walk towards the lift, then returned to the room which Jake was sharing with two other post-op babies.

'You're off duty,' Jasmine Wells, who'd relieved her, reminded her.

'I promised Shelley I'd stay with Jake while they get away from the hospital for a while.'

'As if he'd know whether you were there or not,' Jasmine scoffed. 'That kid's the best sleeper we've ever had in here. But if you're going to watch him, that leaves me free to do the rosters for next week. You OK working nights over the weekend or have you got a hot date with Theo?'

Lauren smiled.

'I don't do hot dates,' she reminded her friend. 'You know full well the only reason I've been seeing Theo from time to time is that he's been trying to persuade me to go to the States and do a perfusionist's course. He keeps pulling info off the internet for me.'

She paused then added, 'And I have to admit I'm

tempted. However, it would mean such a change, and up-rooting Joe, not only from school but from all the other activities he enjoys.'

'He'd adapt,' Jasmine said. 'You know he would. In fact, he'd probably love it, especially if you could get into a school close to one of the Disneylands. Think about that! Then think about all those gorgeous American doctors we see on TV—think about them.'

'Go and do the rosters,' Lauren said, waving her hand to chase Jasmine away, afraid if they kept talking she'd admit just how much she wanted to do the course. Well, not how much she wanted to do the course as such, but how much she wanted a change in her life.

Now she did sigh, but baby Jake didn't notice, and, having let go of a little frustration with the release of air, she shook off the vague feeling of depression that had been hovering around her lately. It was Jasmine's fault. Only two weeks ago she'd announced her engagement, while the week before Becky, the unit secretary, had decided on a wedding date. It felt to Lauren as if the love fairy was back at work, not only in the hospital but right here in the unit. Last year it had touched the lives of three couples connected with the unit and now it was back, the malicious imp, sprinkling love dust willy-nilly.

Thankfully none had landed on her.

Her fingers tingled and she remembered the man who'd shaken her hand the previous afternoon.

'As if!' she muttered to herself, knowing such a man was probably married with two point four children, and even if he wasn't, why would he be interested in her? And then there was Joe.

So she *was* thankful the love dust had missed her.

Of course she was. She nodded confirmation of this to the sleeping Jake. If thinking about studying in the US was causing her major confusion, how much more confusion would love cause?

She gave the baby a wistful smile.

It would have been nice to have remembered love…

Then love was forgotten as she realised all was not well with Jake. A swelling on his hand where a cannula was sited suggested his vein had collapsed. She pressed the help button, knowing whoever was manning the central monitor would call a doctor, and began to disconnect Jake's leads from the monitor.

She would be the monitor while she took him through to the procedures room—to the machine responsible for seeing he kept breathing.

CHAPTER TWO

JEAN-LUC was leaving the unit, his mind on coincidence and betrayal, when he all but collided with the crib a nurse—*the* nurse—was pushing out the door.

'Good grief, you're the doctor who rescued Joe! What on earth are you doing here?'

'So your memory's not all that bad,' he snapped, as the pique he'd been feeling since she'd failed to recognise him surfaced. 'I'm one of the new visiting surgeons on Alex Attwood's team.'

He tapped the ID that was clipped onto his belt.

'Thank heavens—just who I need,' Lauren said, ignoring his jibe and smiling happily. 'You do seem to have the knack of being in the right place at the right time. Jake's vein's collapsed and he'll need a new catheter put in. I'm just taking him through to the procedure room. I've asked Jasmine to put out a call for a doctor, but as you're here, you can do it.'

She manoeuvred the crib into the small room and, though busy reattaching monitor leads to the monitor in there, she continued talking.

'It would happen when I've sent his parents away from the hospital for the first time since he was born!'

Although he knew a collapsed vein wasn't life-threatening, Jean-Luc's training kicked in and he washed his hands then bent over the infant, checking his size, seeing the chest scar of a recent operation.

'Fill me in.'

Lauren was unwrapping a fine-bore cannula, but she responded to his abrupt order without pause. A good nurse…

'Jake Appleton, coarctation of the aorta. Phil caught the case. He tried prostaglandin to keep the ductus arteriosis open, heart medication, diuretics, but Jake continued to suffer congestive heart failure. Cardiac catheterisation with balloon angioplasty to widen the aorta didn't work and in the end Phil had to operate to remove the narrowed section. Jake's been doing well, until this.'

Lauren stepped back, but although her eyes should have been on Jake she found she was now studying the doctor who bent over him, his hands firm but gentle as he lifted Jake's limbs, searching for a viable vein in the baby's already over-taxed and -treated body. Every touch assured her this man not only knew what he was doing but had an instinctive rapport with his little patients.

She couldn't possibly have met him before. His eyes were blue, she knew that now, while as for the rest of his face—well, further scrutiny confirmed the opinion she'd formed yesterday. He was definitely unforgettable!

So presumably she'd met him as Alex had taken him through the unit on a guided tour of some kind. Lauren was aware there were two new staff members, one French—this one, from the accent that curled around his words—the other from South Africa. Both would be working in the unit for six months, improving their skills and no doubt passing on their own expertise to Alex and Phil's surgical teams.

'Problems?'

Phil Park, the head of the second surgical team, arrived but Lauren could see the new doctor had already sited the cannula and was reattaching the drip.

'Collapsed vein,' Lauren said to Phil. 'I could see the fluid leaking out beneath his skin. Dr…'

She looked from the man, still bent over Jake, to Phil, then back to the man.

'I'm sorry, I've forgotten your name.'

The newcomer muttered something under his breath and Lauren, who talked quietly to her charges all the time, assumed he was speaking to Jake. She turned to Phil, who answered for her.

'Fournier,' he said. 'Jean-Luc Fournier. Actually, you'll probably be seeing him around as he and Dr Sutherland, the South African surgeon who is also joining us, will be living near you in the flats at Number 26.'

Satisfied the cannula was sited safely, Jean-Luc had remained bent over the baby, wanting to see the fluid flowing again before he was one hundred per cent certain. With babies' tiny veins…

But as Phil said his name, Jean-Luc looked up, interested in Lauren's reaction—hoping to see shame that she hadn't recognised him the previous day, perhaps guilt that she hadn't been in touch with him after the typhoon—wanting to see something!

Anything!

But the green-brown eyes that met his held no hint of embarrassed recollection, just politeness as she nodded.

'Ah, that explains it,' she said, then turned her attention back to Phil. 'I met Dr Fournier yesterday—he rescued Joe when he was knocked over on the footpath.'

To Jean-Luc she added, 'Thanks for coming to the rescue so promptly.' She smiled. 'Again!'

Jean-Luc felt his body respond to that smile and knew that responding to her was even more impossible than finding her. How could this be after ten years?

Was it leftover lust?

Not a thought he could pursue when Phil was talking to him, thanking him for stepping in.

'You'll be a useful chap to have around,' Phil finished, waving his hand for Jean-Luc to precede him out of the room.

Jean-Luc swung back towards Lauren, but she was once again fiddling with monitor leads, no doubt detaching them preparatory to taking the infant back to the PICU.

Who was she now?

And why was he wondering?

She was married, with a child—end of story!

Or was it?

Surely something of the woman he had fallen so deeply and desperately in love with still lingered within her.

His thoughts left him so unsettled he wanted to go back in and look at the babies in the unit but he was expected upstairs.

Consultations awaited…

Had some of the love dust landed on her after all that she was going weak-kneed whenever the new surgeon was around? Lauren wheeled Jake back into the big room and reattached his monitor leads, thankful Shelley and Brian had missed the little drama, forcing herself to think of them, not of blue eyes that had looked, almost angrily, into hers.

No, she had to be imagining the anger. He couldn't possibly be angry that she didn't remember some chance meeting they'd had earlier, although it could only have been within the last few days—the new team members hadn't been here all that long.

And her memory wasn't usually *that* bad!

It was a puzzle but not one she needed to bother with right now. Although the image of possibly angry blue eyes lingered in her mind and she was distracted as she listened to Brian and Shelley thank her for sending them away, the walk, Brian assured her, having done them both the world of good. Now he would sit with Jake while Shelley had a sleep, and Lauren could go home to sleep herself— No, she couldn't! It was consultation day. She had to sit in on Alex's consultations before she could go anywhere.

She sighed but hurried through to the locker rooms to have a wash and run a brush through her hair, which had been knotted up under the scarf all night. Her face was pale and she smeared some lipstick on her lips then put some on her finger and rubbed it into her cheeks. It didn't help much but she looked less ghostly and hopefully more proficient. Alex insisted on at least one member of the nursing staff sitting in on pre-op consultations because he believed the parents were more confident if they already knew the nurses who would be caring for their infant or child. But seeing a colourless ghost might make them less, not more at ease…

'I'm just explaining to Jean-Luc why we have a nurse sitting in,' Alex said, as she met up with him and the Frenchman outside the door of his consulting room.

'As well as being reassuring for the parents,' Alex continued, 'it helps that the nurse—Lauren in this case—knows exactly what we intend to do in the operation. The parents never take it all in at once, it's just too much for them, and we've found, prior to an op, they are so strung up that they forget what they do take in, so if the nurse can explain to them afterwards, or at least answer their questions, things go a lot more smoothly.'

'For the parents,' Lauren explained. 'They are such an important part of the equation and if they have to wait to see a doctor to ask their questions, then the doctors get overworked and the parents get over-anxious and the situation becomes fraught.'

Could she really not remember him?

How would she react if he said *India*?

Jean-Luc knew he should be concentrating on what he was being told, not on the lack of recognition in the beautiful eyes that met his so trustingly.

'It is so sensible, the idea of the nurse sitting in, I am surprised other places do not do it,' he managed, glad he could be honest—it *was* a good idea—even though he was distracted.

'Coffee first,' Alex declared. 'While we drink we'll run through the list of patients we'll be seeing this morning so you both have some idea of what lies ahead. Lauren, I know you're white with one. Jean-Luc, how do you take your coffee?'

'Straight black, no sugar,' Jean-Luc replied, then was surprised when Alex left the comfortable consulting room.

'He will get the coffee himself?' Jean-Luc asked Lauren, who grinned at him in reply.

'Not used to men getting the coffee?' she teased, the smile still playing around her soft lips.

Jean-Luc shrugged, too busy watching the smile and fighting his reaction to it—not leftover lust at all, but attraction, still alive and well—to answer.

'Actually,' Lauren continued, 'he'll go to the reception desk out front, pick up his pile of case files and ask Becky, the unit secretary, to organise some coffee.'

'Ah!'

The man smiled and Lauren felt a totally inappropriate response. It was deep down in her belly and it felt shivery and hot at the same time, then shock that she could react to something as innocuous as a stranger's smile rushed through her.

Jasmine had a theory that unused emotions and responses grew slack and lazy, like unused muscles. It was a theory she'd propounded often to Lauren, urging her to go out more, to find a man to have a bit of fun with—even sex. 'Because sex is just so good for you—for your general well-being and for your skin—it makes you glow,' Jasmine would usually add, glowing herself because obviously her sex life was very satisfactory.

But Jasmine's theory must be wrong, because there was nothing slack or lazy about the response in Lauren's belly. Or in the way her skin heated, and the tiny hairs on her forearms prickled with awareness…

Jean-Luc saw colour rise in her cheeks, barely visible beneath the freckled olive skin, but there, nonetheless.

Did she remember him?

But, if so, why deny it?

Because she was now married to Joe's father—that would be the most likely explanation—and having a lover from the past come back into her life would be awkward.

Except that awkward wasn't the vibe he was getting from her. Anxiety, yes, as if he worried her in some way, but not the way an old lover would.

Although they were alone together, so surely this was the time—

'You really don't remember me.'

He cursed himself the instant he'd said it, hearing it like an accusation, although he hadn't intended it to be.

She frowned at him, genuinely puzzled.

'Did we meet properly before yesterday?' she asked, and he felt his lips tighten and a frown drag his eyebrows together.

'I'm not talking about recent meetings,' he growled, then regretted his stupid anger—he couldn't *make* her remember—as she looked upset.

The soft, full lips spread to a hesitant smile. 'Have you been to Australia before? I know I've never been to France.'

Her bewilderment was genuine—he had no doubt about that—and hurt pride brought anger in its train.

'Not France—India,' he said, far too abruptly, then caught her arm as the flush faded from beneath her skin and she seemed to stagger. She steadied herself, withdrew a little so he was no longer touching her, and her dark hazel eyes met his with a mix of apprehension and entreaty.

'You were in India? You met me at St Catherine's?'

The words were little more than a hushed whisper, but the desperation he heard in them was reflected in her eyes. Why?

Was the memory of India—whatever memory she did have—so horrific? Of course it would be! His own memory of the typhoon was confused, disjointed, then blurred by pain, but she, who'd been buried alive…

'Did you—?'

The whispered words had barely left her lips when Alex strode back into the room.

'Coffee's on the way and the first patient is in fifteen minutes so we'll skip quickly through these files while we drink it.' He dropped the files on his desk, and pulled two chairs close to it so they could all see the records as he leafed through them.

'Alex, I—' Lauren began, then she shook her head and added, 'The files, of course. Let's get on with them.'

But she shot another look in Jean-Luc's direction, a searching look that turned to despair before she shook her head again and dropped into one of the chairs by Alex's desk.

Jean-Luc took the other chair, too close to Lauren, so he was conscious of the tension in her body and of her attempts to relax, breathing deeply, holding her hands clasped tightly in her lap to still their trembling.

Once she had trembled in his arms, but this reaction—this was pain or fear or something else he couldn't understand.

He cursed himself for upsetting her so badly at the beginning of a working day, but why *was* she so upset?

'Sorry, Alex, I know I've got to stop blaming jet-lag but I was distracted again. Would you please tell me the child's name once more?'

Jean-Luc forced himself to set all thoughts of the past aside and concentrate on what Alex was saying—after all, these would be his patients very shortly. An operation was only the beginning of some children's relationship with their cardiac surgeon—follow-up visits might go on for years.

'Cain Cardella. He was brought to the hospital with aortic stenosis. A balloon catheterisation at the regional hospital failed and we did an open-heart op to repair the aortic valve. There were complications with his coronary artery as well, but he came through the op well and now he's back for a twelve-month check-up.'

Alex passed the file to Jean-Luc, who opened it and

began to read, surprised to see that the 'complications' Alex had spoken of so casually had been quite complex, with the left coronary artery having to be repositioned.

'It was quite a long operation,' Alex said, apparently reading Jean-Luc's surprise. 'Very tricky, but as you will see, Cain's done surprisingly well.'

Coffee arrived and the three of them continued to work through the patient files, Alex giving Jean-Luc a précis of each patient's problem while Lauren added information about the families of the children.

'Now, this one,' Alex said, when they'd reached the final file, 'will be yours. Unless Annie has the baby early, I'll still be here, but I've been reading of your success with the latest septal occluder. We've never used this particular device so we'd all like to see how you use it and to learn why you prefer it. We'll discuss it further at a full unit meeting prior to the op, but for now the patient, Jeremy Willis, is four years old. The specialist who was seeing him over at the Children's Hospital had already decided he'd need to do a closure, then he heard you were coming and contacted us to ask if we'd get you to do it.'

Alex passed the file to Jean-Luc and as the new unit member took it in his long, slender fingers and began to read through the information, Lauren seized the opportunity to study this man who had, so suddenly and surprisingly, announced he'd known her in India.

Not that she hadn't studied him—surreptitiously—earlier. Her reaction to his smile—his touch—had been so extreme, she'd taken every opportunity she'd had to have a good look at him, trying to work out why he affected her as he did.

Was it the scarring here and there on his cheeks—an

accident at some time, which would explain his limp—that added an extra something to the man's appeal? Made him look more attractive?

Fascinating!

Manly!

She shook her head. Theo was a manly man—gorgeous, in fact—but he didn't raise goose-bumps on Lauren's arms when she brushed past him, or make her stomach feel squirmy and uneasy just sitting next to him.

Perhaps it was some fragment of memory in the bit of the past that had never come back to her that made Jean-Luc so appealing.

Had he known her well, or simply met her in passing? Surely it must be the latter, or he would have said more when they'd met the previous day.

Had he been, perhaps, one of the backpackers she'd written about in her emails home—young people who'd sometimes called in and spent a night at the mission, doing jobs around the place in return for shelter and food?

Or had he been something more?

Fear, apprehension and despair all gripped her heart, squeezing it hard enough to cause physical pain in her chest.

Though, doing the maths, Jean-Luc Fournier would have been in his late twenties ten years ago and there was no way such a man—a worldly, handsome, French man—would have looked twice at the lanky, freckly, immature twenty-one-year-old she'd been.

The fear subsided though apprehension remained, useless anger building from despair that she *couldn't* remember!

'So, are we ready? Can I buzz Becky and ask her to send the Cardella family in?'

Alex's question interrupted Lauren's tortured thoughts,

and she thrust away the nightmare of a past that was a total blank to concentrate on the present.

'I'll go out and bring them in,' she said, hoping movement would ease the tension in her body and help her mind focus on her work. Even better, she could show them in then take an unobtrusive seat at the back of the office, away from Jean-Luc and his disturbing physical presence.

Jean-Luc watched Lauren leave the room, surprised that the way she moved, treading lightly and lithely, should still be so familiar to him. Surprised that his body could still react to that movement.

'She's a first-class nurse.'

Startled out of his reverie, Jean-Luc turned back to Alex, trying to read what lay behind the casual comment. Had Alex seen something more than casual interest in Jean-Luc's observation of Lauren? Or was Alex, as word in the paediatric cardiac surgical world had it, omnipotent?

Alex's face revealed nothing—in fact, he was no longer looking at Jean-Luc, but at Cain Cardella's file.

Zut! You must forget Lauren and concentrate on what you are here for, Jean-Luc reminded himself, pulling Jeremy Willis's file from the bottom of the pile and opening it, needing something on which he could focus his full attention.

Then Lauren was back with the patient and his parents and the consultation fell into such a familiar pattern Jean-Luc was swept along, listening, talking, asking questions, learning all he could of each and every patient and the problems the team had been called upon to fix.

'Jean-Luc will be the major surgeon for Jeremy's operation,' Alex explained to Rosemary Willis two hours later when the consultations were drawing to a close. 'I will be assisting but Jean-Luc has more experience with the new type of closure we are anxious to try.'

Rosemary frowned as she looked from Alex to Jean-Luc.

'I don't want you doing experimental things on Jeremy,' she said, speaking quietly so the little boy, whom Lauren had drawn into a corner to play with blocks, didn't hear. 'You must have tried and true ways of closing this hole, so why would you use something new?'

'In the past,' Alex explained, 'in a case like Jeremy's, we stitched the hole up, or put a patch in there. We cut the patch from some other tissue in the patient's body so that made another wound that had to heal. In order to get in there, we had to do a major operation, opening the patient's chest, then putting him or her on the heart-lung bypass machine and opening the heart. With the new occluders, it can be done through cardiac catheterisation, which is much less invasive surgery.'

'He's had cardiac catheter stuff already,' Rosemary said, turning from Alex to Jean-Luc. 'They put a tube up from his groin into his heart to see the hole when he was a baby. If you can do this now, why didn't they do it then and save him all this trouble?'

Jean-Luc smiled at her.

'You would think it would have made sense,' he said, speaking gently for he could feel the woman's agitation and understood it. 'But quite often these defects will right themselves during the first three years of a child's life—in fact, about eighty per cent of them close of their own accord before the child is two. You must see it would be better if Jeremy's body had fixed the problem than if we interfered too early.'

Rosemary nodded, but her eyes strayed to her son, who was knocking down the towers of blocks with great gusto.

'It is such a worry,' she murmured.

'Of course it is,' Jean-Luc said, although his mind had been diverted for a moment as Lauren had lifted the little boy onto her knee and had bent her head close to his, whispering to him—making him smile. Lauren's dark hair had fallen forward and the image of the woman and child reminded Jean-Luc of a stained-glass window in the cathedral near the hospital back at home.

What was he thinking?

How could he be so easily diverted?

He turned his full attention back to Rosemary.

'But you must realise the operation we plan for Jeremy will be far easier on him than a full open-heart operation, and in France we have been using this occluder for several years now. In America there are others which have also been used successfully, so you can be sure Jeremy is not being used as an experiment.'

But if he was expecting instant approval he was disappointed. Rosemary studied him for a moment then turned to Alex.

'You agree this is best?' she asked.

'Not only agree but recommend it. In fact, I would choose that option and do the catheterisation myself but with Jean-Luc here we have someone who has performed it many times, and I am anxious to watch and learn from him.'

'What do you think?'

Rosemary directed her query at Lauren this time.

'A catheterisation is so much less invasive than open heart surgery, it's a no-brainer,' Lauren responded. 'We do caths in the lab beside the ward all the time, it doesn't even need the theatre, although for Jeremy I would think they'll use a theatre because there'll be a full team on hand as everyone is anxious to learn.'

'You're really such an expert?' Rosemary demanded, turning back to Jean-Luc.

He smiled at the anxious mother.

'Modesty should prevent me saying so but, yes, in this particular procedure I am,' he said, knowing she needed re-assurance more than anything. 'I use a yardstick—that's the right word?—to judge operations before I suggest them to a parent. I ask myself, would I do this—use this method or that treatment—on my own child, and if I can answer yes, then I know it is the right thing to do.'

'Oh, you've got children yourself? That's so good to know!' Rosemary said, reaching out and taking Jean-Luc's hand in both of hers and squeezing it. 'Then I will trust you to do what's right for Jeremy.'

It was only when Jeremy wriggled off her knee that Lauren realised she'd been holding the little boy too tightly, her hands unconsciously tightening their grip when Jean-Luc had mentioned children.

Of course he'd have children—didn't most men in their late thirties? She'd already figured that out.

And why should she care?

Because she found him attractive?

Or because he knew her from the past?

Surely she hadn't been thinking he might be the one…

She shook her head at the appallingly ridiculous thought. He was French, sophisticated, gorgeous—hardly the kind of man who would have been smitten by her young self!

'I'll see Mrs Willis and Jeremy out,' she said, getting up and taking Jeremy's hand, then adding to Rosemary, 'Becky will make the appointment for Jeremy's procedure and give you all the information you need for his hospital stay.'

She's escaping, Jean-Luc thought, then he wondered why he would think such a thing, and what there was to escape? *'T'es fou!'* he muttered to himself. He must stop thinking about Lauren—or letting thoughts of her divert his mind from the work he was there to do.

'Do you spend this much time with all your patients and their families? If so, how do you find time for your other work?'

'We find time spent with patients and their families pre-op pays off in the long run. These kids are going to be put through terrible trauma and it's agonising for their families. The more the families know what to expect, the better they seem to handle it, so it's time gained in the long run. Of course, parents are still very distressed when they see their child post-op, but if they understand as much as possible about the procedure they are able to accept that, of course, it knocked their infant around.'

Jean-Luc nodded. He could understand the thinking, but most of his experience had been in major hospitals where time taken to talk to parents was a luxury they sometimes couldn't afford.

'It is a system I would like to set up in the new unit at home,' he said. 'And I like the idea of the nurse being there. Rosemary turned to Lauren for further reassurance before she agreed, and if it is Lauren who will care for Jeremy before and after the procedure, then there is already a small bond formed which will make it easier.'

Alex nodded.

'All the nursing staff are good with the parents, but Lauren seems to have a special talent in winning confidence. Perhaps because her own child has heart problems, although only the families who get close to her would learn about that. Other people must just sense it.'

Alex's explanation echoed in Jean-Luc's head, making no sense because his brain had been blocked by three words— 'child' and 'heart problems'. Little Joe had heart problems?

Heart defects were not uncommon in children with Down's syndrome, so why was *he* upset?

Because it was another burden Lauren had to bear?

Surely not!

CHAPTER THREE

THE consultations over, Lauren headed home, distracted by the idea that the new surgeon on the team had known her in India. The irritation of knowing so little and needing to learn so much more niggled at her as she tried to sleep, and distracted her later as she talked to Joe about his day, and helped him make plans for the local Cubs' sock drive. Together they drew a map of the places he could visit. Many of the houses in the area were divided into flats, so without going too far afield Joe could knock on a lot of doors. But with that done, the thought of Jean-Luc Fournier living just up the road began to burn inside her.

It was no good—she had to know more. *Had* to! Had to talk to the man to see if he could unlock the secrets of the past.

Would he be at home? It was eight o'clock. Would he have had his dinner?

Didn't Europeans eat later?

Certainly they'd eat later than people with nine-year-old boys in their family.

Although he had children himself…

She phoned her mother who lived in the flat above hers, far enough away for her and Joe to lead independent lives but close enough to be there for Joe when Lauren was working.

'I'm just going down the road, Mum,' she said. 'Something I need to talk about with the new surgeon. Can you watch Joe?'

Her mother agreed to come down, used to the fact that, with the strong medical contingent in the neighbourhood, people popping in and out of each other's houses was quite normal.

Lauren let her mother in and was about to walk out the front door when she realised she was still in the old clothes she'd pulled on when she'd got home from work.

So?

She shook her head but raced back to her bedroom where she grabbed her favourite jeans and a dark green top that Theo had told her made her eyes look greener.

Stupid, stupid, stupid. The words echoed in her head as she showered and rubbed herself dry. They grew louder as she brushed her hair until it shone, and louder still as she smeared foundation over her freckled skin, and touched lip-gloss to her lips.

But what was wrong with looking as attractive as she could?

She had no answer, although the excitement that had begun inside her when she'd decided to visit her new neighbour was now turning to a fluttery feeling in her stomach.

More akin to panic than excitement.

The make-up was for courage, she decided as she let herself out of the house and headed for number 26.

But make-up or not, her footsteps faltered and doubts grew like mushroom clouds in her mind.

He probably won't be at home.

She pushed her feet along the pavement, her reluctance now mixed with fear.

He might not know.

That was what was really worrying her.

For ten years that part of her life had been a blank—retrograde amnesia caused by a hit on her head. And though most of her memory had returned over time, the period immediately preceding the injury—six weeks, her mother had told her—remained tantalisingly hidden away.

What puzzled the doctors was that it was such a long period of time. It wasn't uncommon for memory of the twenty-four or even forty-eight hours preceding a head injury to be lost, but six weeks?

It might be due to some earlier trauma just before she was buried under the bricks, they suggested, but to Lauren that was hardly reassuring.

Now here she was, about to talk to someone who had been there. But did she really want to find out what happened—did she want to fill in all the blanks?

She did and she didn't…

She *had* to!

Pushing open the gate to 26, her hands trembled.

'Of course you want to know—you need to know,' she told herself, angry that she was becoming so emotional about it. 'And, anyway, he might not be able to tell you much—he might only have been passing through.'

'Ah, so you still talk aloud to yourself.'

The voice made her turn, to see Jean-Luc, green supermarket shopping bags dangling from his fingers, standing right behind her. She stared at him, unable to take in not the sight of him but the words he'd spoken. It wouldn't have been more shocking if the camellia bush by the path had spoken.

'You know that?' she whispered, stiff with fear and a weird reluctance.

'Come on, move along, don't block the path!'

A woman's voice! The tall, blonde beauty was right behind Jean-Luc, so Lauren had no choice but to step off the path and let the couple pass by with their groceries.

She looked behind them, expecting to see the trailing two point four children but none appeared, although knowing the new surgeon was married was a very different thing to supposing he would be.

'Neighbourly visit?'

Good grief, now Theo was there, too, jingling his car keys in his fingers. The whole situation had rapidly developed into a farce. How could she possibly talk to Jean-Luc with his wife and half the hospital around?

Well, with his wife and Theo around!

'Come in, Lauren. I must put things in the refrigerator then we will have coffee. I have bought a coffee-pot among my purchases, and promised Theo coffee for his kindness in taking us to the shops.'

Jean-Luc had set his shopping bags down to find the key to unlock the door and, having opened it, stood aside to let the blonde go into the house.

Lauren hesitated, visualising the scene, herself and Theo sitting at the kitchen table while Jean-Luc and his wife put away their groceries and made coffee. Hardly the perfect opportunity for Lauren to ask him if he'd known her lover.

Her stomach squirmed and a fluttery panic filled her chest.

Could she *ever* ask such a question?

Of *anyone*?

Even of someone who might understand and be sympathetic about her amnesia?

And then there was the fear of actually hearing an answer to the question—of *knowing*!

For nine years now Joe had been hers and only hers—all right, so she shared him with her mother and Russ and Bill, but really he was hers. If she knew Joe's father, wouldn't she *have* to tell him he had a son? And if she did, what if he rejected Joe?

How could she then live with the knowledge that she'd loved a man who couldn't love his son?

The permutations and combinations of it all were endless and so worrying she knew she should just turn around and go home, then possibly move to Melbourne—or go to the US and do a perfusionist's course!—so she wouldn't see Jean-Luc and wonder just how much he knew…

Her soul cringed at the thoughts that raced through her head, but she couldn't stand by her neighbour's front path all evening. With a sigh that didn't begin to relieve the tension in her body, she followed Theo into the house.

Someone had flicked on the lights, but even without them Lauren would have been able to find her way around—the houses in the street all followed the same design, and even when they'd been divided into flats, the flats were similar, except in her case there were three flats, her brother Russ and his partner Bill occupying the top floor, that would, in the larger houses, have been servants' quarters. All the flats shared a common entry and a foyer from which the stairs rose. The ground-floor flats had a doorway opposite the stairs and it was through this door Jean-Luc led the group.

'The best thing about these places is the size of the kitchen,' Theo said, as he and Lauren entered the big room. 'Makes an ideal congregating space.'

If I'd wanted a congregation, Lauren thought bitterly, I'd have gone to church, but she didn't allow her lips to move.

It was disconcerting enough to have been caught talking to herself once this evening—and by someone who obviously knew of her habit.

The someone in question was stacking purchases into the refrigerator, and she watched him, staring at the way he moved, at his profile, his hair, the way dark hairs curled around his wristwatch, seeking something, *anything*, that might trigger a memory—some movement or glimpse that might give her a clue that would open the doorway into the past.

Nothing!

'Like that, is it?' Theo whispered to her, as he drew out a chair for her to sit.

'Like what?' she snapped, but quietly, not wanting to draw the other man's attention to this conversation.

'You fancy him.'

'I do not!' Lauren shot her tormentor a look she hoped would quell him, but all he did was grin, his dark eyes dancing with delight that he'd found a way to tease her. 'And, anyway, why are *you* here? To talk shop with Jean-Luc? Or because of his gorgeous wife? Where's she gone, by the way?'

'That's not his wife—that's Grace, and her flat is upstairs,' Theo told her, and at that moment the woman in question returned.

'Grace, it seems you've not met your neighbour. Lauren's a nurse in our unit, and she lives next door but one. Lauren, meet Grace Sutherland, visiting surgeon from South Africa.'

It couldn't be relief that flooded through Lauren, yet some strange emotion had certainly disturbed her equilibrium while the glances Jean-Luc shot in Lauren's direction from time to time were making her regret more and more her decision to visit.

'Well, I've got my things put away—so coffee,' Grace declared. 'You promised us real coffee, Jean-Luc.'

'Oh, please, don't worry about coffee for me,' Lauren said, feeling more uncomfortable by the minute. 'I just called in to…'

Talk to Jean-Luc! She could hardly say that, because Grace seemed like the kind of woman who would ask why.

'To see if there was anything you needed, or anything I could do to help you settle in. I really should be going.'

She stood up, moving so quickly she tipped over her chair. Theo bent to set it upright, but Jean-Luc was there before him, picking up the chair then touching Lauren's arm.

'Stay for coffee,' he said quietly, but the words meant little, her mind too busy trying to process her reaction to his touch.

It had been nothing—a couple of his fingers brushing against her shoulder—yet it had galvanised her senses to such an extent that she *had* to sit down, her knees no longer reliable enough to hold her up.

Was Theo right? *Did* she fancy the new surgeon?

If only she could remember what fancying someone felt like! Had her nerves tingled and her skin thrilled to her lover's touch? Had her knees gone weak and wobbly? Was that how Joe's father had made her feel?

Or was her reaction to Jean-Luc nothing more than her apprehension about what she might or might not learn from him—and into what dark depths that information might lead her?

Grace joined them at the table, leaving Jean-Luc fiddling with a silver coffee-pot, spooning aromatic coffee grounds into it, but most of his attention was on the unexpected visitor. She looked pale—ill almost—certainly stressed.

He wondered if bad things had happened in her life in the last ten years.

Could things have been so bad she could no longer remember happy times? For they *had* been happy times that he and she had shared. Blissful times when love had blossomed in such unexpected circumstances they'd both decided it was their own special St Catherine miracle.

Until the letter.

'Is French coffee-making always such a ritual?'

Grace's question cut through his memories and he hurriedly put the pot on the stove to heat and busied himself finding cups, milk and sugar, then setting out biscuits for his guests.

But as he placed the plate of biscuits on the table, Lauren stood up, more carefully this time so her chair remained upright.

'I'm sorry, I really can't stay,' she said. 'Perhaps another time!'

And she rushed out the door, her sandals slapping against the parquet flooring in the hall, the opening and closing of the front door finalising her departure.

'Is there something wrong with that woman?' Grace asked, turning her attention to Theo.

'No, there's nothing wrong with Lauren but you'll find the other members of the unit are protective of her. Apparently she had quite a severe head injury when she was younger,' Theo responded. 'I don't know the full story but she was in her early twenties when it happened and she was in a coma for some months. Although it left no permanent brain damage she still suffers headaches and some memory loss, I believe, and she changed her career path from medicine to nursing because it would be less stressful.'

Head injury!

Coma?

Amnesia?

It was as he had guessed.

The coffee-pot was spluttering on the stove, the liquid hissing as it overflowed onto the hot plate, but Jean-Luc was lost in the past. He'd shepherded Lauren and a lot of the younger children into the church before the worst of the winds had struck, thinking the brick building would be the most solid place for them to wait out the typhoon. Only later, when he had been in hospital half a world away, surgeons piecing his leg back together, had he learnt that the church had been destroyed. And all this time he'd believed Lauren was dead, for how could anyone have survived the collapse of such a building?

No survivors, he'd been told, and he'd grieved for his lost love.

'Excuse me,' he said, knowing he had to speak to her again to sort this out. He hurried from the room, Grace's protests joining the sizzle of the spilling coffee as he strode along the passage to the front door.

But once there he hesitated, again aware of the dilemma that faced him. If Lauren was happily married, or even in a relationship. Joe had mentioned a mum, Gran, Russ or Bill being at home. He remembered that Russ was Lauren's brother's name, so Bill? Children did sometimes call their fathers by their first names.

And if she *was* married—no doubt happily—what right had some stray Frenchman to burst into her life, forcing memories she might not want to resurface in her mind?

Although she had come to visit him.

It *had* to be to ask him about the time they'd met before.

If *he* had lost his memory of a part of his life, he would want to know…

He opened the front door then shut it again, wondering if he could go back to the kitchen and ask Theo for more information about Lauren. Though he couldn't as that would amount to gossiping about a colleague, something he hated.

Besides, he could hear Grace's clear voice coming from that direction, complaining about volatile Frenchmen who never seemed to know what they were doing. Going back into the kitchen would confirm her statement. He opened the door again and this time he walked through it, closing it behind him. He looked up at the night sky, pleased the darkness of the park across the road meant he could see the stars, although these were different constellations here in the southern hemisphere, unfamiliar shapes and patterns in the brightness.

And Lauren?

Once, for six short weeks, she'd been the brightness in his life—his moon and stars. They'd made promises and shared dreams but now were strangers. Must they remain that way?

Must they meet as nothing more than colleagues?

He had to find out more—find out, for a start, about her marriage and her child.

If she already had to carry the burdens associated with a child with heart problems, did she need whatever chaos his reminding her of the past might cause?

But who to ask?

He took a walk around the block, passing number 30, then went back inside 26, to find Grace and Theo no longer there, his flat deserted. A note informed him they'd gone across the park to get some decent—underlined—coffee from the café.

Relieved to be alone, he took out his laptop, searching for articles on amnesia. He knew the clinical details of it, but wanted specialist psychiatric opinions and papers—did sufferers benefit from filling in the blank spaces in their memory, or could the knowledge they learned be harmful?

Opinion, as ever in medical fields, was divided. More often than not, he discovered, most people, over time, recovered most of their memories. The parts that remained missing were usually only the actual details of the trauma they'd suffered and the events immediately preceding them. But for Lauren to not remember him meant she must have a blank of at least six weeks…

And if she was married…

He sighed with frustration, as the more he learned the less he seemed to know.

Although she *had* come to visit, and he was fairly certain she hadn't come to repeat her offer of neighbourliness.

The following morning he took up his position by the window yet again, telling himself he wasn't spying, or watching for Lauren so he could walk to work with her.

But he was.

It had struck him in the middle of a restless night that walking to work with her—meeting her casually on the way—could prove the best way to talk alone with her.

The little bus pulled up and Joe, floppy hat crammed down on his head, came out the gate of 30 and boarded it, then the front door opened once more and a tall man Jean-Luc had noticed the previous day emerged.

Russ or Bill?

Studying him more closely, Jean-Luc noticed that the sun had brought out red highlights in the man's dark hair. Russ?

Perhaps talking to Lauren's brother would be better than talking to her—at this stage, anyway. He might be able to find out about her current situation and so gauge whether or not his revelations would be harmful to Lauren.

He hurried to the gate, nodding a greeting to the tall man with Lauren's colouring.

'You're one of the new surgeons,' the stranger said, holding out his hand in the friendly fashion Jean-Luc was coming to accept was the Australian way. 'I'm Russ Henderson. My sister Lauren is a nurse in your PICU.'

Jean-Luc introduced himself and fell into step beside the man he wished to interrogate. Although he had to be careful it didn't sound like an interrogation, or even a probe. Somehow he had to find out as much as possible about Lauren without appearing obvious.

And he had absolutely no idea how to go about it!

'You're French, I hear,' Russ was saying. 'Never been to France—well, not what you could call going to France. I spent some time in the UK and did the obligatory weekend trips across the Channel, but that was in my student days and apart from the inside of bars I saw very little and remember even less.'

'It is expensive for Australians to travel, given that your country is so far away from other continents, yet I see and hear of Australians travelling all over the world. It is hard to comprehend.'

Russ laughed.

'I think perhaps it's because we *are* so far away from

other places that we have the urge to travel. And in my family, my mother always encouraged us to travel. I spent a year in the US when I was still at school as an exchange student and Lauren spent some months in Japan, then, when she finished university she went to India, wanting to work with people she felt were less privileged than she was. By that time I was in the UK, although I came home when…'

He stopped and turned towards Jean-Luc.

'But you don't want to hear the history of our family. Tell me about yourself. What brought you to Australia— was it just the opportunity to work under Alexander the Great or something more?'

Or something more?

The phrase rang in Jean-Luc's head.

He'd tried to tell himself it wasn't something more, yet deep within he'd always felt it was something he had to do.

Not that he could tell this man that he'd come to lay his sister's ghost to rest.

Especially when that sister wasn't dead!

'Alexander the Great—you call him that?'

'People who work with him tease him with the accolade. Being the modest man he is, Alex hates it.'

'I imagine he would,' Jean-Luc said politely, while his mind ran through things he might have said.

Your sister worked in India?

I worked in India.

I knew you sister in India.

All were far too intrusive—he'd never make a spy. Talking to Russ had been a stupid idea. He would have to restrict himself to politeness.

'You work at the hospital, too?'

From then on it was easy, Russ talking about the chal-

lenges of caring for people in intensive care, Jean-Luc discussing his experiences in the French equivalent.

'You must come to dinner one day,' Russ said, as they
crossed the road to the hospital. 'I'd like to learn more
about the way they do things over there. You can never
know too much in my caper—although I guess it's the
same with you. That's why you're here.'

It was a throw-away remark, and Jean-Luc ignored it,
although he suspected memories of Lauren's descriptions
of her home city had subconsciously helped him choose.

'See you later,' Russ said, as they parted at the lifts.

The words brought Jean-Luc back to the present and he
smiled at the man who was Lauren's brother.

'We say *"à bientôt"* which is much the same, but now
I will speak Australian. See you later,' he said, and, still
smiling, he entered the lift, pressing the button for the floor
that housed the PICU.

Lauren wasn't there, but he refused to let that bother
him. He had come to see the babies before he began his
day. Lauren would contact him again—he was sure of that.
Just as he was certain she didn't want to discuss the past
in front of others—which was understandable given she
was undoubtedly in a relationship and had a child.

'Theatre meeting in ten minutes—do you know where
to go?' Maggie Park, Phil's wife and one of the anaesthe-
tists on the two teams, was standing by the centre console
in the unit, and greeted him as he came out of the big room.

Jean-Luc nodded. Alex had explained the routine when
he'd shown Jean-Luc through the operating theatres, em-
phasising the fact that their work in theatre went more
smoothly when the whole team was in on the briefing. So,
in ten minutes, they would all gather in the small lecture

theatre and Alex would run through the operations scheduled for the day. A PDA first. Closing the ductus arteriosis that allowed flow of blood from the pulmonary artery to the aorta of a foetus, a simple operation and a good one to start the day.

He was thinking about that—about why, in some newborns, the ducts didn't close themselves—as he walked to the lift, and wondering why Alex had chosen to operate rather than close it through cardiac catheterisation, so he didn't notice the lift doors open, or realise Lauren was among those who stepped out until she was right in front of him.

'Jean-Luc,' she said, his name so soft on her lips he barely heard it. 'I wondered— Do you think—? Would it be all right…?'

The unfinished phrases lost what little momentum they'd had and she just stared at him, a desperate plea in her ever-changing eyes.

'Could we talk sometime?' she finally managed.

'Of course,' he said, hurt by the measure of tension he could see in her eyes and feel in her body.

'Alone?'

'Did you miss the lift or were you waiting for me?'

Maggie came to stand beside him, and Jean-Luc touched Lauren on the arm.

'Of course,' he said. 'I will get in touch with you.'

He was trying to ease her concern but at the same time shield her from Maggie's interest.

'The Willis child,' he said to Maggie, amazed to find the name of the patient coming into his head at precisely the right moment.

But as Lauren departed, and he stepped aside to allow

Maggie to enter the lift in front of him, Maggie sent him a look that suggested she'd seen right through his charade.

'She's a lovely woman,' she said, and although she didn't say any more about Lauren's troubled life there was a warning implicit in the words.

How could he possibly get in touch with her? He didn't have her phone number, and the last thing she wanted was to draw attention to herself or him within the unit.

Lauren pondered these problems as she returned to the unit, then switched her mind from personal matters to work. This was what she did—it was her life, or a major part of it—and the past, with its hidden secrets, had to be firmly put aside.

But Jean-Luc had known her…

She shook her head, thinking that might clear it, and settled in front of a computer to check the progress all her young charges had made during the night.

He said he'd contact her, and something in the way he'd touched her arm—something in his dark blue eyes—had suggested he was telling the truth. So there was no point in her worrying about how he might achieve that, was there?

Mollie Ashbury was due to be transferred to Special Care—good for Mollie, graduating so quickly. Lauren stood up. She'd check Mollie first, check out any special needs Alex might have written up, then arrange for her to leave their care.

Work! It not only took her mind off imponderables but it brought her real pleasure.

Alors! It was all very well telling Lauren he would contact her, but how?

Ask her to have dinner with him at the Italian restaurant across the park?

And what would her husband—Bill?—think of that?

No, he had to arrange something private yet casual—a chance meeting. The canteen! No reason why she shouldn't be eating at a table and he could join her—they were colleagues after all.

He was deciding this as he walked home through the dusk after five hours in theatre, agreeably tired but excited that he'd actually felt like part of the team as they'd done the PDA, then a much longer operation to sort out a transposition of the great arteries on a six-month-old baby who had been flown in from one of the Pacific Islands. To his surprise, the parents had been French-speaking, so he had stayed on after the others left the hospital to talk to them and, hopefully, lessen their fears for the baby's future.

He arrived home and was considering what to have for dinner—would he cook or go across the park to a restaurant?—when the front doorbell rang. Remembering Lauren's visit the previous evening, his heart gave a little leap. But when he opened the door he found Joe, not Lauren, standing there, smiling uncertainly, the dog called Lucy standing by his side, eyes fixed on Jean-Luc.

I am the guard!

'Hello again,' Jean-Luc began, looking up the path and along the footpath, thinking, as it was getting dark, the child shouldn't be out with only the dog for protection—although Lucy's watchful eyes suggested she was all the protection Joe needed.

'Hello,' the boy replied, his thick tongue making the word clumsy but still easily recognisable. 'I am Joe. I am a Cub!'

He'd obviously learned this introduction and he pronounced it proudly. Jean-Luc felt a jab of sympathy for Lauren that she had the extra responsibility of bringing up a child with a disability—although, judging by Joe's self-assurance, she was doing a wonderful job.

Jean-Luc smiled at the little boy in his blue polo shirt with its yellow collar and yoke, the knotted scarf around his neck a give-away that it was the Cub uniform. Joe smiled back and handed him a plasticised sheet of paper.

"'I am Joe Henderson,'" Jean-Luc read aloud from the sheet. "'My Cub group is having a sock drive.'"

At the word 'sock' Joe produced a handful of socks from a satchel over his shoulder and tried to spread them across his chubby hands.

'Socks,' he said. 'I am selling socks.'

He beamed at Jean-Luc, proud and excited to be trusted with such an important enterprise.

'Come in,' Jean-Luc offered, thinking it might be easier to look at socks in a proper light. He had no doubts about buying socks—not only was this Lauren's child but Joe, with his winning smile, was utterly charming.

Joe shook his head.

'I mustn't go inside houses, that is rude,' he told Jean-Luc. 'Just outside and just these houses, and only with Lucy.'

Lucy, hearing her name, bared her teeth in what might have been a smile but still held a suggestion of warning.

Joe took back the card, which went on to explain about the sock drive to raise money for the local Cub group, and turned it over, pointing to a map drawn on the back, with some houses marked with red crosses.

'Friends of Mum's,' he said. 'From work. My mum's a baby nurse.' Joe's tongue might have stumbled over some of his words but he radiated pride, his love for his mother shining in his blue eyes.

'I know her at the hospital,' Jean-Luc said. 'And of course I'll buy some socks. How many pairs can I have?'

'Twenty?' Joe said hopefully.

An innocent or a good salesman?

'How can I wear twenty pairs when I've only got two feet?' Jean-Luc teased gently, but Joe was not to be deterred.

'Bill says socks are very good Christmas presents,' he said.

Bill again?

'And who is Bill?'

Jean-Luc asked the question before he could get too hung up over the ethical issues of questioning a child about his mother's life. In the context, he assured himself, it was kind of all right to ask.

'Bill's my friend!'

Serves you right! Jean-Luc admitted to himself.

'Well, Bill's right,' he said. 'Socks make very good Christmas presents. I *will* take twenty pairs.'

CHAPTER FOUR

'THAT'S Mum!'

Busy writing his order in an order book that had also come out of the satchel, Jean-Luc barely noticed the first call, but when Lauren called again he answered.

'He's here!' Jean-Luc moved off the porch and waved to Lauren, who was standing at her front gate.

She came swiftly towards them, her anxiety evident in the sharp tone she used as she scolded Joe.

'It's nearly dark, Joe. You know you should come home before it gets dark.'

'But John was buying socks,' Joe protested, while Jean-Luc looked from the child to his mother and, as the attraction that had been there from his first meeting with Lauren sparked again in his body, he wondered about Bill.

'You don't *have* to buy socks.' Lauren, more disturbed than ever in Jean-Luc's presence, hastened into speech. 'I'm sure you can buy wonderful socks in France.'

'One can never have too many pairs of socks,' her colleague replied. He turned back to Joe. 'What else do I need to write down?'

'You write your name and where you live and how many socks you want,' he said.

Lauren watched as Jean-Luc filled in the order form. Watched closely, trying to work out why this man affected her as he did—trying even harder to remember him.

It was useless! There was nothing at all familiar about him, and if she'd ever felt these strange internal reactions to him before—well, she couldn't remember that either. But she doubted she'd have been reacting to the man's attraction at the time when she'd been in love with Joe's father, so maybe, back then in the blank space in her life, her body hadn't warmed, and her skin hadn't tingled when she'd seen Jean-Luc Fournier.

Could she ask?

Not about her reaction to him, of course—there'd be no mention of that and hopefully it wasn't showing—but about the blank—about the time they'd met before. Mum was at home—she could send Joe to her place for his dinner, and perhaps have a talk with Jean-Luc.

Although being alone with him would undoubtedly make all the strange manifestations of attraction she was feeling far worse. And did she really want to know—to fill in the blanks?

For Joe's sake, yes. He was entitled to know who his father was.

'There, that's done.'

Jean-Luc handed the order book back to Joe, who thanked him politely then looked at the paper.

'Wow! You really *are* buying twenty pairs. My six will beat the others.'

'You don't need to buy twenty pairs of socks,' Lauren protested, staring at the man she didn't know. 'What on earth will you do with them?'

She knew she was talking to dispel the uneasiness that

churned inside her whenever she was near him, but her
question brought a smile to his face and the uneasiness
turned to heat.

'I can give them away as Christmas presents. I have
it on very good authority that socks make excellent
Christmas presents.' He paused, studying her, while Joe,
delighted with his order, and with Lucy at his heels, headed
up the path and turned towards his house.

Lauren watched them go and knew she had to ask, waiting
until Joe was safely inside the gate at home before turning
back to the man who was causing her so much turmoil.

'Did you know me at the orphanage?' The question
blurted from her lips before she could dither any more.

The dark blue eyes looked gravely into hers.

'Yes,' he said, and the word, though as forceful as a
punch in her stomach, was not enough, the tension in her
body tightening so much her muscles ached.

'I hit my head. I don't remember— You must have
thought me rude—not recognising you. It's so hard.'

The disjointed scraps of information spilled into the
gathering darkness, and she knew she had to do better. She
took a deep breath and tried again.

'Did you work at the orphanage? Were you a volunteer
there—or were you one of the backpackers who stayed a
night or two then moved on?'

She studied his face, the scarred skin, the strong planes
of cheekbones, the jut of chin, desperately seeking a
glimmer of recognition—some hint of remembrance.

'I was there, but your memory loss... I don't know
much about amnesia. Are you sure you want to know? Are
you sure it won't be harmful? Hurt you in some way?'

He seemed hesitant, even emotional, yet she must be

picking up the wrong vibrations. What reason did such an assured man have to be uncertain?

And did his uncertainty matter when she was on the point of filling in that terrible blank space once and for all? Of finding out who'd fathered Joe?

Although that question brought its own fear in its train…

'I *have* to know,' she whispered.

He reached out and touched her arm.

'Of course,' he said, his voice as strained as hers had been. 'But here it is impersonal, the flat…'

Jean-Luc hesitated. It wasn't going to be easy to talk anywhere! How did you tell a woman she'd been your lover once?

So where? They could hardly sit over coffee in the restaurant across the park, talking as if it was a normal conversation. And the park at night—the lighted areas were busy with people exercising, the other areas possibly dangerous?

And how could telling of the past in words even in part relate the rapture they had shared, the delight, the tenderness, the passion…

Did he tell her all of that?

His own tension was bad enough yet he was sure he could feel Lauren's radiating from her body, filling the air around them with high-density vibrations.

This was impossible!

They needed somewhere they could both feel relaxed.

'In India we often walked on a beach,' he said, touching her lightly on the forearm, hoping touch might soothe her, if only slightly. But touching her was not a good idea. Apparently, the chemical arrangements in their bodies that had first sparked their attraction were still alive and well— the attraction far from dead.

T'es fou! He had to pull his mind into order.

'You talked of a beach near where you lived. We shared a liking for beaches for I, too, lived by the sea, although in a village, not a suburb. Is your beach far away? Would it be possible to go there? To walk together on the sand while we talk?'

He was still holding her arm so he felt at least some of the tension drain from her body.

'Coogee? I told you about Coogee? I *must* have known you well!'

She smiled with such sincere delight Jean-Luc felt his stomach knot. Would she be equally delighted to learn the rest of what he had to tell her? Or would she, like he, be simply thrown into more confusion?

'It's a short drive away,' she told him. 'I'll just duck home and ask Mum to take care of Joe, then get the car and pick you up.'

But as she moved away the sensor light in the porch came on and Jean-Luc saw the smile slide from her face. Yes, she might be glad to think some of the spaces in her memory would be filled in, but she, too, was dubious—perhaps even afraid—about just where more information might lead her.

But then her parting words echoed in his head. She would tell 'Mum' she was going out—Joe's gran, not Bill, though maybe Bill was at work, which would explain Gran babysitting.

And, really, it was none of Jean-Luc's business whom Lauren had to tell—or whether she was married to or otherwise involved with this Bill.

So why did it bother him?

Because he still felt the tug of attraction towards her—that's why.

The small car pulled up in what seemed an incredibly short few moments later, but perhaps he had been dreaming—thinking back to how things might have been had not a typhoon struck the village where they'd worked. The interior light came on as she leaned across and opened the door for him, and he saw apprehension—close to fear—in the way her skin clung tightly to the bones of her face and in her almost colourless lips.

'Tell me what you do remember,' he suggested, when he'd shut the door and buckled his seat belt.

She sighed, her eyes on the road as she pulled out into the traffic.

'Nothing—not one solitary thing. Not even flying off to India, although Mum and my friends tell me there was a great send-off at the airport.'

She braked for a red light and turned towards him.

'I think that's the hardest part, not being able to remember emotions. I can imagine that I was feeling happy and sad at the same time—there at the airport. Excited yet apprehensive because I'd found out about St Catherine's on the internet but had never spoken to anyone who'd ever been there. Mum told me all this, and then there are emails I sent home to family and friends and they tell me what I did—or some of the things I did—and I sound as if I was having a fantastic time, so why can't I remember it?'

Recalling what he'd read about amnesia, Jean-Luc was intrigued.

'What do the experts say? I assume you've seen specialists—neurologists?'

The lights turned green and she drove on, her concentration on the road and the moderately heavy traffic.

'Plenty of experts, and most of them have differing

opinions. In the beginning, when my brother Russ flew to India from England where he was working and found me in a hospital two hundred miles north of St Catherine's, I remembered nothing—not who I was, nor him, not even Mum when I got home, yet the weird thing was I remembered how to do things—like clean my teeth.'

She negotiated her way around a large van and turned down a side street, then slid a smile towards Jean-Luc.

'I was very suspicious of Russ at first. I'd assumed I was Indian and here was this Australian trying to take me away. He had to wait until the consular department issued a replacement passport for me, then show me mine and his and the names and addresses on them both.'

The road dipped and ahead Jean-Luc could see the darkness of the ocean, although any beach was hidden by the tightly packed buildings that must stretch along the shoreline.

'So, Russ took you home?' he prompted, as they stopped again at traffic lights.

'Not straight away, because the doctors didn't want me to fly for a while. So we went to stay in a holiday village by the sea—a long way from St Catherine's and the devastation of the typhoon. Then one day when we were walking on the sand, I had what seemed like a vision. I'd been playing on the beach with Russ when we were kids. I'd built a sandcastle and he knocked it down and I cried and cried. I asked him if that was true and he hugged me hard and danced and shouted, and all the quiet, gentle Indians around us on the beach thought he was a madman. But it was true and from then on little bits and pieces came back until I could fit most of my childhood into place, and my teenage years, even my years at university.'

The traffic was moving again, and she stopped talking,

but Jean-Luc knew her mind was more on the past—on that blank space in her life—than on the route they were taking to her beach.

'And India?'

'All I know about it,' she said softly, as she turned the car and they started down a hill to where he could finally see the shoreline, and the white foam of the waves that advanced and retreated on the beach, 'is what Mum and Russ and my friends at home could tell me from the emails I'd sent them before the typhoon struck.'

Alors! She hadn't told them about him—hadn't mentioned his name or surely it would have been familiar to her. Had he then been so unimportant to her?

Even with the emotional detachment ten years had brought, he found it impossible to accept. He'd been so in love—and was sure she had felt the same.

'Here—the beach—Coogee. Did I tell you the name?'

She'd parked the car and was looking at him, uncertain again, anxiety making her voice shaky, although she was doing her best to hide it.

'You did,' he answered, but now they were at the beach he wondered why he'd suggested it. Far off on the horizon the moon was rising, sending a silver path across the ocean, right to where white foam flecked the tops of waves and the water washed with a soft shushing sound on the sand.

The scene demanded romance, not devastating revelations, although need the revelations be so devastating?

They'd been lovers—didn't everyone have a youthful romance somewhere in their past?

'Lauren,' he began, so uncertain now his nerves were taut, his muscles tight with anxiety, 'are you sure about this?'

She stared at him, and in the light from the streetlamps beyond the car he saw her frown.

Then smile!

'Not at all,' she murmured, the rueful grin still hovering around her lips. 'In fact, I'm terrified. But…'

She stopped as if deciding not to tell him whatever it was she'd been about to say, adding only, 'I need to know.'

But how much? That was Jean-Luc's problem. It seemed she knew about the kind of work they'd done, for those things would have gone into her emails home. In that case, what other information would she be after?

And why?

'Shall we walk?' he said when silence suggested she'd said all she could say right now.

She opened the car door by way of reply and turned in her seat so her legs dangled out, enabling her to slip off her sandals. Removing his shoes and socks and turning up the legs of his trousers took Jean-Luc a little longer, and maybe he didn't hurry as he wanted to get his body back under control and give his mind time to come up with some easy way to tell Lauren what she needed to know.

Actually, telling her wasn't the hard part—working out what they would both do with the information afterwards was what blocked his thinking processes.

Perhaps chat would help.

'So this is Coogee,' he said, as his feet touched the sand beneath the promenade. 'You used to laugh because I said a letter to Jean-Luc Fournier, Cassis, France, would always reach me. You said you doubted a letter to Lauren Henderson at Coogee, Australia, would get to you.'

She paused and looked at him and, seeing her face, the beautiful planes of it, the deep-set eyes, he was transported back to that other beach, where they'd walked, and talked, and kissed.

And he wanted to kiss her again—so badly he could feel his body trembling with the need to hold her, touch her, taste her lips.

'Did you try?'

She obviously wasn't talking about kisses. His mind tracked back and he moved closer and took her hands.

'No, I didn't try, Lauren. I, too, was injured. When I regained consciousness I was told that you had been killed.'

He took a deep breath to chase away remembered pain, then added bluntly, harshly, 'I thought you were dead!'

She moved away so he had to drop her hands, and shook her head as she stared at him.

'I was dead to you for all those years, then you see me on the street. You must have thought you'd seen a ghost.'

Her reading of the situation was so exact he felt a little of his tension drain away.

'I've definitely had ghosts haunting me the last few days,' he admitted.

'Poor you,' she said softly, while huge dark eyes scanned his face and it seemed to him she was trying to read his thoughts when, more likely, she was still trying to find something in his features she remembered.

Finally, she lifted her hand and placed the palm against his torn and puckered skin.

'These injuries? Your limp? You were badly injured?'

'Bad enough to be repatriated home on a medical flight then to spend three months in and out of hospital—but that's a long time in the past and we're not here to discuss my injuries.'

'But of course we are, it's part of what I want to know,'

she said. 'Three months is a long time—does your leg still bother you? Should we sit and look at the ocean rather than walk?'

'We're not walking yet,' he said, but he turned to walk, because standing close to her—close enough for her to cup his cheek—was so disturbing he couldn't marshal his thoughts into sensible order.

Couldn't think at all, in truth, because all he wanted to do was touch her, hold her, kiss her…

Because she's a symbol of the past—of a time when you were happy—that's all, his cynical self suggested.

But cynicism didn't stop the wanting.

She caught up with him, and her question—'So before the typhoon separated us, were we friends?'—suggested she was far less affected by this reunion than he was.

And why would she be affected by him if she was happily involved with Bill?

Lauren told herself she had to pretend this was nothing more than the fact-finding mission she'd requested. She had to ignore the moon on the water, the shushing of the waves on the beach, the salt tang in the air and all the other ingredients of romance, and just talk to this man.

And more important than banishing the ingredients of romance from her thoughts, she had also to ignore the totally extreme physical sensations the man awoke in her. How could she have touched his cheek, knowing that being close to him was enough to make her knees weak, so touching him would surely be far worse?

It had been! As her hand had curved around that scarred skin, she'd felt her body come alive, sparks of what could only be desire shooting along her nerves, rioting in her blood and making her bones go soft and gooey.

Embarrassed by her own reactions, she'd blurted out the question as she'd fallen into step beside him, and when he didn't answer she turned to look at him, seeing his face in profile, shadowed—seeing still a stranger.

So why did her body respond so forcefully?

'Yes,' he finally answered, but his strides had lengthened so she had to hurry to keep up with him and barely had the breath to tell him that a single affirmative was a very unsatisfactory answer.

'Just yes—is that all you have to say?' she managed, and he stopped walking and once again turned to face her.

'What else do you want me to say, Lauren? That you were special to me? Is that what you want to hear?'

His voice was harsh, scraping against some emotion in his throat.

'Is it important you know details of a past romance, now you're happily settled with another man and a child?'

A past romance?

The shock was like a physical blow and possibly because her mind was unable to fully process it, she latched onto the end of his sentence.

'There's no other man,' she said, heat rising to her cheeks when she realised how lame that sounded.

And how pathetic!

'But there is a child!' he said. 'You can't deny that!'

He sounded angry and hurt and—betrayed? Surely not! She was imagining things, but nothing in her imagination had ever prepared her for what Jean-Luc Fournier had, in fact, revealed.

That this man who'd come quite by chance into her life—this French surgeon here to work with the team—was Joe's father!

Or was that what he'd said?

She sorted through the words in her head.

Past romance? Special to him?

He hadn't exactly said they were lovers.

Yet she was reasonably certain Joe hadn't been an immaculate conception and if she'd only been in India six weeks…

Hell! Things were getting worse and worse, although a past romance might explain why she was feeling what she was feeling whenever this man was near. Somehow he'd imprinted on her body, like baby geese imprinted on a human as a mother.

'You've nothing to say?' he demanded, coming closer to her, facing her, still sounding angry.

'I was thinking about geese,' she said, as the imprint thing made her bones go weak again.

'Oh, geese, of course. What else would you be thinking of on a beach in the moonlight with a man who has just told you that once he loved you?'

'You didn't tell me that—just that I was special,' she protested, still unable to accept where the information might lead.

'Then I'll tell you now,' he said, his voice very deep and very quiet so she had to lean a little closer to hear him. 'I loved you, Lauren, and when I heard that you were dead, I wished to die myself. I grieved for you and for what we might have had.'

The words were ragged, as if they'd been torn from him against his will, and unthinkingly she again touched his cheek, then she leaned closer and whispered, 'I'm sorry that you had such pain.'

She hadn't meant to kiss him, but right then it seemed

the only thing to do—to kiss him better as she kissed Joe better when he was hurting. Except she couldn't think of Joe right now.

Couldn't think at all because Jean-Luc Fournier was kissing her back, hard and hungrily, devouring her lips, demanding a response, kissing her as she had never, in her memory, been kissed before.

She'd kissed him on the cheek, a sympathetic gesture, nothing more. But Jean-Luc Fournier didn't accept sympathy from anyone so he'd moved his head and his mouth had captured her lips—parted in shock but still with the power to heat his blood and send it thundering through his veins.

He felt her respond and the kiss deepened, until he no longer knew if he was kissing the Lauren of the past or this new Lauren. One thing was for sure, she was real, not a ghost at all, and he felt a burning desire building inside him, desire that wasn't a memory but very real, and very, very urgent.

Mon dieu! He had to get a hold on himself.

He broke away and strode towards the waterline, aware of the shock Lauren must be feeling but not wanting to remain near her lest the urge to take her in his arms—to comfort her—proved too great.

Lauren lifted her hand and touched her fingers to her lips, trying to recapture the feel of his mouth on hers.

Hell's teeth! Was she really standing on the beach at Coogee thinking about a kiss when that man had just rocked her world? Or had he? Was telling her he'd loved her the same as telling her he was her lover? *Was* he Joe's father? Dear heaven, what was she to do? What was she supposed to feel?

Not hot and trembly and excited, that was for sure!

They had to talk. She had to explain about Joe!

Or did she?

The man was French—he was here for a short time—what would happen with Joe when he left?

What if he wanted Joe, or worse—what if he *didn't* want Joe?

Totally confused, and definitely uncertain which option would be worse, she followed him slowly down to the water.

'Were we lovers?' she asked, standing in the soft sand, water washing over her feet.

He swung around and took her hands again.

'Lauren, I have no idea about amnesia apart from what I learned in medical school a long time ago and what I've read in books and gleaned off the internet since Theo told me last night you'd been injured. I don't know whether knowing things is good or bad for you. Neither do I know what you need to know.'

She looked into his face, shadowed on one side, the other lit by the pale silvery light of the moon.

'I would like to know it all,' she said softly, 'or that's what I've always thought, but I realise now that knowing things isn't the same as feeling them. And while you can tell me things, how much will they mean if I can't remember how I felt and what I thought at the time?'

She sighed and moved away.

'Will knowing you were my lover, if that's the case, make me remember how a kiss felt back then, when I was twenty-one and fairly new to kissing?'

Jean-Luc stared at the woman who stood, arms crossed protectively over her chest, staring out at the silver path of the moon across the water. And in the pale light he saw the tears coursing down her cheeks, and guessed that such silent tears must come from pain deep within.

A man would have to be carved from stone to not respond. He went to her and put one arm around her shoulders, then, with infinite tenderness, he wiped away her tears.

'It may not be the same, not after ten years, Lauren, but this is how a kiss between us feels,' he murmured, moving so both his arms encircled her, loosely in case she felt trapped or wished to escape, then he bent his head and kissed her without the heat of the previous caress, feeling her lips pliant but not responsive.

He drew her closer and deepened the kiss, his tongue exploring her lips, telling himself he was simply trying to tease some memory to life within her, while his body heated again in response to the inexplicable but undeniable attraction that had sparked between them from their first meeting.

She pushed away—not immediately, but soon enough to make him feel a twinge of guilt that maybe he'd been taking advantage of her. Then she smiled.

'I imagine kissing you was what got me into strife in the first place,' she said, and although her voice was teasing her eyes were clouded with doubts and worry. 'It *was* you?' she added. 'You *were* my lover?'

It seemed a strange way to ask for confirmation, puzzling, but he could think about that some other time. Now all he could do was nod, so much emotion roiling through his body he doubted his ability to speak—and certainly not to speak in English. But now she was frowning.

'But you would have been older and no doubt experienced,' she protested. 'What did you see in a fairly inexperienced young woman from Coogee Beach?'

That was easy to answer, for only the truth would do.

'I saw an honest, caring, beautiful young woman, excited by all the sights and sounds around her, willing to take on any job no matter how dirty or menial. I saw a woman who gave and gave of herself, offering love to those orphan kids in so many ways—in a touch, a cuddle, a walk on the beach, a song at bedtime—countless things. You were, and probably still are, very special.'

She shook her head as if to deny his words, repudiating them so they hung, perhaps slightly foolishly, in the air between them.

'That is true,' he added, wanting her to believe him. 'My question, though, back then, was what did you see in me?'

That seemed to startle her and she studied him for a moment, then smiled.

'An outrageously handsome man, I would think,' she said, still smiling. 'And French as well! To a far from sophisticated Sydney girl, you must have seemed so—so worldly?'

'We were friends as well, not just lovers,' Jean-Luc said, somehow needing to reassure her there had been more to their affair than simple lust. But was lust ever simple? He was feeling something now and although he didn't want to label it as lust, he certainly didn't know this new Lauren well enough for it to be anything else.

'I'm glad about that,' she said, turning away from him and walking along the beach, staying on the wet sand where the tail ends of waves could wash across her feet as they encroached and then retreated in their ceaseless movement.

Lauren moved, thinking if she was further from this man she had known but didn't know now, she might be able to think straight, but he joined her, walking beside her, not too close, but near enough for her to be aware of him in every cell in her body. This was the man to whom she'd given herself—the man she'd loved. How could this be, that they could walk like this and, yes, she could feel attraction, but not know how she'd felt before?

And the attraction was dangerous, for it would blur her thinking and think was what she had to do. Think about Joe and what knowing who his father was might mean—to her, to him, and certainly to Jean-Luc.

He didn't look at her as he walked so all she could see was his profile, lit by the moon. Strong nose and determined chin, the scars, barely visible, causing a slight pain in the region of her heart.

But right now she didn't want to be feeling things—her emotions were too chaotic to cope with the manifestations of attraction. Perhaps if she found out more about the past—found more pieces of the jigsaw she was no closer to putting together.

Apart from the fact she now knew who had fathered Joe and she certainly didn't want to go there right now!

'As ex-colleagues and friends, can we talk about what happened—not with you and me but in the typhoon? You talked of an injury—what happened to you?'

They'd reached the rocks at the far end of the beach and as they turned he put an arm around her shoulders. A friendly arm—a colleague's arm—or so she told herself, although the effect it had on her nerve endings suggested differently.

'We had a warning that the storm, as they first labelled it, was sweeping across the bay but were told it would cross the land several hundred miles to the south. The staff at St Catherine's had procedures for such an emergency and they secured storm shutters and made sure everything outside that could blow about was brought inside. Then the storm veered off course and the waves built until even without the radio warnings we could see it was going to hit the village. When the first wave of water swept across the orphanage grounds, the priest in charge suggested we move the babies to the church, which, being brick, should withstand an onslaught better.'

He paused but, hard though Lauren pressed her mind to remember, no images returned.

'You and I carried the babies over there, and we made a little nest for them beneath the altar. You stayed with them…'

He drew a ragged breath and moved away, as if touching her might make it all too real.

'I was helping the older children build barricades when the big wave came. I saw the church crumble and collapse and knew you were there beneath it all.'

Hearing his pain—the anguish he must still feel—Lauren moved towards him, putting her arms around him and holding him tightly.

'You did what you thought best and I escaped,' she reminded him, but she didn't ask about the babies for Russ had found out details for her and she knew many children and infants had perished.

He returned her embrace and they stood together, seeking solace and reassurance from the close physical contact.

Then, subtly, the chemistry of it changed, and this time it was Lauren who initiated the kiss.

Exploratory, she told herself, excusing her boldness in pressing her lips against Jean-Luc's. Experimental, even.

But excuses were soon forgotten as the warmth even a casual touch from this man could generate spread throughout her body and his lips joined hers in exploration and experimentation and just plain kissing.

Plain kissing?

Surely plain kissing couldn't leave you breathless?

Couldn't make your body quiver with some emotion you couldn't understand, let alone name?

Her lips opened to his demands and the kiss deepened until Lauren could feel the heat of it right down to her toes.

This was folly! There was so much to be sorted out. But if this man could make her—a mature woman—feel this way, how much more intoxicating and entangling would his kisses have been to her twenty-one-year-old self?

Eventually he drew away and, embarrassed by the heat of her response, Lauren hurried up the beach. They weren't even at the hospital and the love dust was affecting her— that had to be the answer. She had no memory whatsoever of this man, yet here she was kissing him with…fervour, a weird word she'd never used but surely it was the only one that fitted now.

Jean-Luc caught up with her but thankfully said nothing, although perhaps if he had then she could have answered and they could both have pretended the kiss hadn't happened. They climbed the steps to the promenade and as they did so she again noticed his limp.

'Your leg—it was injured in the typhoon. You said three months in hospital. It must have been bad.'

'Pretty bad, but the main problem was that infection set in before I was repatriated back to France so I had operations to remove that and to remove infected bone. Learning to walk again took the time.'

Lauren smiled at him across the car.

'You forgot how to walk and I forgot my lover. What a pair!'

She was deliberately keeping this light-hearted, Jean-

Luc realised as they slid into the car. Then he silently ac-
knowledged that this was good—for how else should
lovers from the past react to each other?

Yet he didn't think either of their reactions to the kiss
had been connected to the past, except as far as it acknowl-
edged the attraction between them still existed…

But attraction was dangerous—he knew that.

Attraction wasn't enough for a stable, long-term relationship, but the strength of it could blur that fact, and
tempt the people feeling it into mistaking it for love.

Lauren was turning into their street—the drive had
seemed incredibly short.

She stopped outside his temporary home and he turned
towards her, reluctant to get out of the car—to leave her—
yet not understanding why.

She was looking straight ahead, her head slightly
bowed, so the dark curtain of hair hung forward, hiding her
face from him. Without thinking, he lifted his hand and
tucked the wing of it behind her ear.

'Has it helped, us talking?' he asked, wondering if his
gesture was so he could see her face as he asked the
question or an excuse to touch her again.

And if it was the latter, why? He didn't know this
woman so was the attraction he felt for her or for a dream?

She smiled but the smile didn't take the worried look
from her face.

'It will help,' she said, turning to face him fully. 'Once
I've got it straight in my head.'

He stared at her, so beautiful in the dim light in the car,
and felt a response that definitely wasn't lust. It caught at
his lungs and squeezed in his chest and he had no idea what
it was but knew it could be dangerous…

CHAPTER FIVE

A SLEEPLESS night was not the best preparation for another day in theatre with Alex's team, but Jean-Luc knew his focus would be solely on the work they were doing, and blessed his ability to compartmentalise his life.

Or so he thought, until he arrived at the hospital—very early because his confusion over his walk on the beach was too great for him to handle a normal conversation with his upstairs neighbour, and he knew Grace was perceptive enough to guess something was wrong.

The first person he saw as he entered the PICU was Lauren.

'On an early shift?' he asked, compartmentalising nicely in his head while his body rebelled, remembering the kiss they'd shared on Coogee beach.

She looked at him—hard—then shook her head.

'Off duty, in fact,' she said, holding out her arms so he realised she was wearing jeans—snug-fitting jeans—and a T-shirt, not a nurse's smock. 'Little Brooke Symonds is having her operation this morning and I knew her mother would be worried so I came in to talk to her and make sure she had breakfast. It could be a long day.'

'Brooke is the TGA? Alex's operation?'

Lauren nodded and led him to where the tiny baby lay sleeping in her cot, wires from the monitors taped to her chest and an oxygen tube feeding into her nose.

'I know with transposition of the great arteries the op has to be performed as soon as possible after birth,' Lauren said, washing her hands in the waterless cleanser beside the crib then touching the baby girl's hand, 'but she's so tiny to be going through major surgery.'

The infant's little hand had curled around Lauren's finger, and Jean-Luc felt a loss akin to pain that he had never felt a child—his child—curl a hand around his finger.

And never would, given the failure he'd made of his marriage and engagement and his determination not to repeat a long-term commitment.

Although, thinking of an infant's clasp on his finger was sentimental nonsense, surely brought on by the emotional discussion he'd had with Lauren the previous evening.

Compartmentalise!

'The sooner the operation is done, the sooner little Brooke will be able to develop normally,' he said, ruthlessly focussed on the present—on work! 'No surgeon likes operating on newborns, mainly because the heart muscle is so weak and— I do not know the word to use in English.'

Lauren smiled at him.

'Phil says soggy. Like sewing Camembert, he says.'

Jean-Luc nodded, unable to reply because his compartmentalisation was failing him and Lauren's smile had made him think things he didn't want to think.

Fortunately more members of the team arrived and the morning ward round commenced, every child examined, every detail of his or her status reviewed, tubes removed or inserted, drug changes ordered, notes taken. Then finally little Brooke was prepared for surgery, her mother accompanying her on the short journey to the theatre where she was given time alone with her daughter.

Jean-Luc watched Lauren, hovering in the background, and knew she was there to support the mother, who looked as young as Lauren had been when he'd first met her. Was it her injury that led her to have such empathy with parents, or the fact that she too had a child with heart problems?

Zut! He was thinking of Lauren again when he should be focussed on what lay ahead. But he was glad that Brooke's young mother had someone with her, someone to lead her back to the parents' room where she would wait through the agonising hours that lay ahead.

How had Lauren felt when told her son had Down's syndrome? *And* had a heart defect? Fool that he was, Jean-Luc had failed to ask what kind of defect, although now he thought about it, atrioventricular septal defects were quite common in children with Down's syndrome.

Had Joe's been fixed?

And though Lauren claimed there was no man in her life, Joe must have had a father, so there had been.

He was wondering why the thought of Lauren with another man would disturb him as much as it did when Theo touched his arm.

'This way,' Theo said. 'Time to scrub. Aldo Stephens is doing the opening—he's Alex's registrar—and personally I'd like you to be ready to step in as well. It's not that Aldo isn't up to speed—he's very good—but if there's anything that can go wrong in an op, it will happen when poor Aldo is operating. The man has a curse on him.'

Jean-Luc pictured the face of the good-looking young man he'd met on his first day—a man who looked more like a rugby player than a surgeon. He thought of baby Brooke and said a silent prayer that today would not be one of Aldo's cursed days.

Inside the theatre, Brooke looked even smaller, her tiny body supine on the operating table, little eyes taped shut, a heavy plastic cage arrangement erected around her so an accidentally dropped instrument wouldn't harm her.

Any harm she suffered would not be accidental, and hopefully the surgery would ensure she went on to live a full and happy life.

'Jean-Luc, hello again,' Aldo said. 'I think you've met all the team.'

And team it was—an inner circle of theatre nurses and surgical assistants, an anaesthetist and Theo near the head of the table, then an outer circle of more nurses who were the gofers, each with their own responsibilities, whether to the surgeons, the anaesthetist or the perfusionist.

Jean-Luc greeted them all in a general way then moved so he was behind Aldo where he could see but not be in the way. When operating himself, he used a stool, as indeed many surgeons did, but today he needed to be mobile so he could duck and weave as the almost balletic movements of an operation swirled around him.

Lauren had led Brooke's mother, Katie, back to the parents' room, but one look at the two couples already inside had made Katie back away.

'I can't go in there!' she protested to Lauren. 'Those women both have men to hold them—seeing them makes me feel worse, not better.'

'What about the canteen? We can find a quiet corner and sit there, have a coffee, talk?'

Katie shook her head.

'I hate the canteen—the smell there makes me feel sick.'

Lauren studied the pale, exhausted-looking teenager in front of her. Only seven days ago Katie had given birth and rather than having the joy of a healthy baby to help her recover from the birth, she'd had one shock after another. No wonder she was looking—and no doubt feeling—fragile.

Neither, as far as Lauren had been able to fathom, did the young woman have any support—no family, no friends, and certainly no partner had been sighted during the time she'd sat vigil by Brooke's bedside.

'Walk in the park?' Lauren suggested hopefully. 'The operation will take hours and the fresh air might do us both good.'

Suspicion flared in Katie's eyes as she studied Lauren.

'Why are you doing this for me? Why do you care?'

Lauren paused. She rarely talked about herself or Joe, but Katie was very young, very alone and at breaking point.

'Nine years ago—actually, it's nearly ten years ago—it was me,' Lauren said quietly, putting her arm around Katie's shoulders and guiding her towards the lift. 'I was luckier than you in that my mum and brother stood by me and were there for me, and lucky because Joe, that's my son, although he had a small heart defect, didn't need major surgery. But he has Down's syndrome and that was a shock. We all expect our babies to be perfect so it's always a real blow when we find out things aren't perfect.'

'What about his father?' Katie asked, but the lift doors opened at that moment and the mass of people inside saved Lauren from answering.

But only until they'd safely negotiated the crossing to

the park and had reached a tree-shaded garden seat beside the small ornamental lake.

'Did his father know? Did he want the baby?'

How to answer? Suddenly, Lauren was faced with questions she hadn't heard for ten years and back then hadn't been able to answer. But now she could and an image of Jean-Luc as he's stood beside Brooke's crib that morning flashed into Lauren's mind.

He'd looked…bereft! That was the only word that fitted.

Because he didn't have a child of his own?

She realised with a shock as sudden as a lightning strike that she knew nothing whatsoever about his current circumstances. She hadn't thought to ask him. She might have been kissing a married man last night!

'*Did* he want the baby?'

Katie's insistence brought Lauren back to the present but it was getting harder and harder to shove her thoughts away.

'I'd had an accident,' she said, wondering whether coincidences really happened or if she was just a pawn in some grand plan of life, suddenly thrust into a situation so impossible it could only have been conceived so the fates could laugh at her. 'I couldn't remember the man, or getting pregnant, or anything.'

Still couldn't remember, even though the past was no longer quite such a black hole, but she didn't say that and was pleased that Katie didn't ask, too caught up in her own misery to want to share Lauren's.

'My boyfriend died,' Katie whispered. 'Before I knew about the baby. But he would have wanted her, I know he would, no matter what Mum and Dad said.'

'Do your mum and dad know Brooke needs this operation?' Lauren asked.

'They don't know she's born even—they don't want to know. They kicked me out when I wouldn't have an abortion.'

'You don't want to tell them?'

Katie shook her head, the misery in her eyes almost too much for Lauren to bear. But she knew Katie would have had a hospital social worker assigned to her, and that person would be trying to find someone to support the young woman. She, Lauren, had to be a friend, although she did need to ask one question.

'What about your boyfriend's parents? Did you tell them about the baby?'

Katie shook her head.

'They were so upset after Darren died I didn't want to bother them, then Mum and Dad did their carry-on and I left town and Mum doesn't talk to Darren's mum—not good enough to be her friend, she reckons, although Mrs Malone is really kind and she was always nice to me.'

'With Darren dead, she might like to know some of him lives on in Brooke,' Lauren suggested tentatively, and Katie turned to her, big eyes wide as if such an idea had never occurred to her.

'Do you think so?'

Lauren nodded then decided she needed to be more assertive. If Mrs Malone was kind—and Katie certainly needed support…

'I do!'

But even as she said it she wondered about Jean-Luc's mother—did she have a right to know she had a grandson? And as suddenly as the image of her sandcastle on the beach had come to her, another image came—no, not an image, but a voice, French-accented, sounded in her ears. 'Do not feel bad for me because I have no siblings, for I have a mother and father, a *grand-mère* and a multitude of *tantes*—aunts—'

She couldn't see a figure, just hear the voice, and as surely as if the live Jean-Luc was standing beside her, telling her these things, she knew he was an only child. If he *hadn't* married and had children, then Joe would be his mother's only grandchild.

'Would *you* tell her for me?'

Lauren dragged her attention back to Katie, although a part of her was so excited over the little snatch of memory. Would more come back? Soon? How much? This was surely Jean-Luc's doing!

'Tell who?' she managed, forcing herself to focus on the distressed young woman.

'Mrs Malone. Darren's mum! I couldn't—not without crying—but you could if I gave you her phone number.'

'Me? Don't you have a social worker who would do it?'

'She's bossy and she doesn't understand. She keeps saying I have to tell Mum and Dad, but they knew I was pregnant and they didn't care then, so why would they care because Brooke is sick?'

Lauren shook her head.

'I suppose I can talk to Mrs Malone for you,' she said reluctantly, sorry now she'd got herself into this mess. Although thinking of Jean-Luc's mother, she felt a twinge of guilt and wondered if, in taking on Katie's request, she might in some way atone. 'But where does she live? This is the kind of thing that might be better told in person rather than over the phone.'

'Thirroul,' Katie replied, naming a seaside village south of Sydney that had become a suburb of the large city of Wollongong. 'Mum and Dad live there, too.'

So Katie hadn't run far from home, and both sets of

parents were close enough to be visiting her and their new granddaughter.

And providing emotional support for Katie!

They walked back to the hospital, Katie happier now, intent on getting the Malones' address for Lauren, hopeful instead of depressed.

'The nurse said I wouldn't be able to see Brooke until this afternoon so I'll have a sleep now,' she announced when she'd handed over a slip of paper with all the details on it. 'I didn't sleep at all last night. Thanks, Lauren!'

Lauren accepted both the paper and the gratitude but Katie's dilemma had stirred up a sludge of emotion in Lauren's head. Joe's rights, Jean-Luc's rights, his family's rights…

She was thinking about all of this when she bumped into him outside the theatre, where she'd gone to find out how the operation was faring.

'Brooke's done, the operation went well, and she's through in Recovery. Is her mother all right?'

Lauren nodded, but as she looked up into his face—into those intense blue eyes—the only thought in her head was that she had to tell him about Joe.

Soon!

Because now she knew he was the father, what reason could she later give for *not* telling him?

'Are you finished for the day?'

'I believe so. Phil is operating this afternoon but Grace is working with him. You are asking for a reason?'

The simple answer was yes, except it wasn't simple at all.

She said yes anyway, adding, 'I'm driving down to a place on the coast south of here, and the views on the drive are magnificent. I thought—you're a visitor—you might…'

Fortunately, as she wallowed in a swamp of half-sentences he rescued her.

'I would love to accompany you,' he said very formally, then he smiled and she remembered all the reasons she shouldn't shut herself into the close confines of a car with this man who had such a powerful effect on all her senses.

But she had to tell him, and in the car—perhaps after visiting the Malones—surely an opportunity would present itself.

'You are visiting friends, perhaps?' he asked as they drove in ever-present traffic through the southern suburbs of Sydney a little later.

'Visiting Brooke's grandparents, although they don't know they are grandparents yet.'

'That would be sad. My mother is forever regretting the fact that I failed to give her a grandchild.'

It was a casual comment as far as Jean-Luc was concerned, but from the look on Lauren's face, she hadn't taken it that way. Or maybe it was the traffic making her frown.

He studied her, wondering if their talk the previous evening had awoken any memories, wanting to ask but afraid of how he'd react if she said no.

Wondering, too, if she was feeling any of the manifestations of physical attraction he felt whenever he was near her—these manifestations so much stronger within her small car.

She'd responded to his kisses the previous evening, but he'd had a feeling that for her they had been experimental—kissing him a test of memory or an attempt to jog something loose in that sealed-up part of her brain.

But as the silence grew and thickened with, he felt, the charges that sparked between them, he had to speak.

'You will visit Katie's parents?'

The traffic had lessened, possibly because they'd turned onto a less busy road and were passing through bushland with strange-looking trees and plants.

Lauren turned towards him and shook her head.

'This is all national park,' she said, waving her hand towards the bushland, although her attention was back on the road. 'Katie's boyfriend was killed in a motorcycle accident before she knew she was pregnant and we're going to tell his parents who also don't know there's a baby.'

Jean-Luc digested this information but it seemed odd to him that Lauren would be doing this, odder still that she would ask him to accompany her and, most odd of all, that she seemed so tense and uptight—far more strained than he would expect someone removed from Katie's family dynamics to be.

'This is part of your job?' he probed, and when she glanced his way this time she grinned at him.

'No, not at all, and no doubt the social worker would disapprove, but I felt these people had a right to know they had a grandchild.'

She paused and took a deep breath, then blew it out between her lips.

'Just up ahead there's a place I can stop—Stanwell Tops. There's a spectacular view—you can leap out over the cliff if skydiving appeals to you.'

She wasn't stopping for the view, or so he could harness a parachute to his back and leap off a cliff. There was something more, and somehow it affected him, for all her talk of Katie and Brooke and grandparental rights!

He felt his stomach tighten but when she did pull into a parking area and brought the car to a halt, he forgot everything but the panorama spread below him, the long line of cliffs and beaches, the blue Pacific Ocean crashing against the rocks below, the white foam of the surf fringing the waves that washed on golden sand.

'This must be one of the most spectacular views in the world, yet one hears of Sydney and the Opera House and Harbour and no one talks of this—so close!'

Lauren had joined him on the viewing platform and seemed delighted at his praise.

'I love it, too, and now we can drive right along the coast. The old coast road slid away in heavy rain and landslides but now there's a new road built like a bridge out over the ocean. Come on, I'll show you.'

Probably instinctively she'd taken his hand as if to lead him back to the car, but though the touch was warm and stirred his blood, he didn't move.

'You stopped here to tell me something,' he said quietly, and knew he'd guessed correctly when colour leached from her face, making her freckles stand out, dark flecks on her pale skin.

CHAPTER SIX

'I...'

SHE stared into his face, desperate appeal in her eyes.

'I thought,' she began again, 'that it would be easy but, honestly, Jean-Luc, I haven't a clue how to say what I need to say.'

She walked away, back to the viewing platform, but though she looked out to sea he doubted she saw anything.

Had she sensed his presence that she spoke as he came up behind her?

'Last night, I told you about Russ finding me in hospital. But what you don't know is that, as well as a concussion and amnesia, I brought home Joe, my son, a tiny embryo who had clung stubbornly to life inside me while I lay as if dead.'

Jean-Luc tried to translate the words into French, sure they'd have more meaning to him in his own language, but his brain had stopped working, the enormity of what she'd told him too much to take in.

She turned now so she was facing him, her eyes pleading for understanding.

'I could have had an abortion—in fact, Russ suggested it, though not because Joe had Down's syndrome. We didn't know that then. He thought, with my fragile state of health and memory loss, it would be for the best. But apart from the fact that I felt anyone who'd managed to hang in there with me deserved a chance at life, I knew…'

She stopped, sighed and turned back to the view before adding in a voice so low he barely heard the words.

'I know this will sound stupid, Jean-Luc, but I knew that I must have loved whoever had fathered Joe. I knew that I wouldn't have—wouldn't have had sex, not casually, not with just anyone…'

Her voice was shaking now, and Jean-Luc understood that. He was shaking, too, the talk, the memories too emotional for his brain to handle so his body had taken over with an automatic response.

'Not with someone I didn't love.'

He stepped forward and wrapped his arms around her. Surely many people had embraced in this place of such beauty, but few, he was sure, would have clung together as he and Lauren did then—for support, and comfort, and because the world they knew had shifted under their feet.

Well, his world had, mightily, and he guessed Lauren's had as well, suddenly finding the father of her little boy.

A man who was a total stranger to her now…

He had a son!

The enormity of it moved him away from her, set him pacing back and forth, the majestic view forgotten as he tried to take in what he'd just heard and make it meaningful.

He pictured the little boy, in his Cub uniform, proudly selling socks.

A *little* boy.

'Joe is ten?'

'Nine—ten in a couple of weeks. Downses are small for their age. The dates compute, Jean-Luc!'

The hurt in Lauren's voice was like a knife wound, but he, too, was hurting that he'd never known his son—held him as a baby, seen his first smile, felt his tiny hand grasp his finger…

He wanted to rage about this, to shout at someone, but it was hardly Lauren's fault that she'd had a concussion.

That she'd forgotten him.

Facts didn't stop him feeling angry.

'Did you try to find out who I was?'

She stared at him.

'Of course I did. Or Russ did—I wasn't with it for a long time. But he contacted every aid agency he could find in that area but all the orphanage records had been lost in the floods and most of the staff and children killed. Father Joe died, I suppose you know that. I'd talked of him so often in my emails and he'd seemed so kind, so wonderful, I named Joe after him.'

'You talked of Father Joe in your emails yet didn't mention me?'

It was something that had been grating on him, so the words came out far more harshly than he'd intended.

Lauren flinched but didn't turn away.

'Do you think I haven't wondered about that myself? Haven't thought about it all the time? I hinted at a romance, said I'd met someone special, but I was so cautious about it that when I reread what I'd written I had to wonder if you were married—if there had been something illicit in our relationship.'

'As if I would do such a thing!' he protested, but then he remembered he had, technically, been married at the time and worry tightened his gut.

Should he tell Lauren about their argument?

But Lauren was smiling know, a sad smile but a smile nonetheless.

'I didn't know you—didn't remember you, remember?"

Then she sighed and shook her head.

'In the end I realised that whatever it was we'd had between us—you and I—it must have been too new and rare and precious for me to share. At that stage, anyway. Maybe later I would have said more, but as it turned out there wasn't any later, was there?'

She sounded lost again and it was all he could do not to take her in his arms and hold her tightly against his body. But such contact was as dangerous as unstable gelignite.

He had a son.

He had to think.

Lauren recovered before he did.

'I'm not telling you this because I want anything from you, Jean-Luc. But talking to Katie and finding out that her baby's grandparents don't know Brooke exists impacted on me to such an extent I knew I had to tell you. Which doesn't mean any more than that. I'm happy to go on being a single parent,' she said. 'I don't have any expectations from you as far as Joe is concerned. It was my decision to keep him, and he is well cared for and totally loved within the family, so you needn't worry about his welfare or feel you have to take responsibility for him.'

She paused, knowing she was talking too much, but so much had happened in such a short time her mind was totally befuddled. She tried again.

'I did want to find out about Joe's father, but only so I'd know some background health stuff, and probably because I felt he should know Joe existed, and know how well he's doing.'

She stopped abruptly for Jean-Luc was scowling at her, making it even harder to put her thoughts into sensible sentences.

'No expectations?' The word's snapped from Jean-Luc's lips as her hurried explanations took form in his head. 'I have a child and you don't expect involvement from me? Is that what you are saying? He's mine but he's not mine?'

Her eyes looked dark as she studied him and he realised she was as lost in this morass of emotion and information as he was.

'We should be going,' she said, her voice sounding strained—exhausted almost. 'Katie phoned Mrs Malone and told her some friends of hers were going to call in, so she's expecting us.'

'So telling Mrs Malone she has a grandchild is more important than talking to me about my son!'

Now he sounded plain grouchy, but Lauren was way ahead of him in the recovery of poise department and greeted his complaint with a shake of her head.

'We can talk in the car. You've met Joe, you know he has a disability, but what you don't know is that he also has tremendous ability as well. He's a bright kid, always happy, and he's sociable, and he loves being part of a group—loves belonging. I'm sorry you've missed so much of his life, but he's far more interesting now than he was as a baby.'

She spoke lightly, but Lauren's heart was scrunched into a tight ball in the middle of her chest, sitting there like a rock so she had trouble breathing.

What if Jean-Luc wanted Joe?

What if he didn't?

And how could two people who lived thousands of miles apart share a little boy?

Had she done the wrong thing, telling Jean-Luc?

The questions crowded in her mind and tightened the fist gripping her heart.

She reached the car and climbed back in behind the wheel, and for all her worry she was still overly conscious of Jean-Luc sitting so close beside her, conscious of him in a physical way, as if his body was giving off rays of some kind that teased her skin and tickled her nerves.

'What kind of groups?'

He was obviously not feeling tease and tickle rays from her.

'Well, school, he loves school. And Cubs you know about. He's also a Nipper.'

'Nipper? This is like Cubs?'

The perplexed look on Jean-Luc's face made Lauren smile, although most of her attention had to remain firmly on the road, which was winding down the cliffside towards the ocean and the bridge that spanned the headlands.

'Nippers are junior lifesavers. Do you know about the lifesaving movement? I guess it's mostly an Australian thing. Young people who voluntarily patrol the beaches during summer. When we get down to Thirroul, after we've seen the Malones, we'll go to the beach—there should be some lifesavers still on patrol.'

'Joe is a lifesaver?'

The incredulity in his voice brought a real smile to Lauren's face.

'Junior lifesaver and, no, I doubt he'll ever graduate to being a real lifesaver, but the lifesavers aren't saving lives all the time, they're watching for sharks and for people in difficulties and they tell people to swim within the flags, and warn them about sunscreen.'

But another glance told her she'd lost him again.

'I'll explain later,' she said. 'Look, here's the bridge.'

And the beauty of the scene was enough to stop Jean-Luc's questions, although as she watched him looking out in wonder at the dark blue ocean, she longed to remember more than just a voice telling her he had no siblings.

Surely if she remembered that, she should remember more. The frustration of it gnawed at her stomach, making her feel physically ill, and deep breathing didn't seem to help, but they were off the bridge and driving through the little seaside villages, built for the miners who'd dug coal out from under the sea in these parts.

'Thirroul—this is where we're going. I've marked the page in the map book there on the back seat. Could you have a look for Tasman Parade for me, please?'

Jean-Luc turned to get the book, his hand brushing against Lauren's arm in the process. Why didn't she have a larger car? Here he was trying to sort his chaotic thoughts into some kind of order and all the while fighting against the attraction that fired the air between them whenever they were close. It was like sitting in the middle of a minefield, aware that one false move could trigger an explosion.

A piece of paper marked the page in the book, but it wasn't just any piece of paper, it was a photo of Joe.

'Did you put this there deliberately?' he demanded, as an emotion he didn't understand punched him in the heart.

She glanced over and he saw her embarrassment.

'Of course not. It's probably been in there for ages and I just stuck it in the right page when I looked up the address today. Bill's always taking photos of Joe and printing them off on his computer—they're everywhere around the house so it isn't hard to pick one up to use as a bookmark.'

'Ah, and so we come to Bill!' Jean-Luc said, pleased to find anger replacing the confusing emotion he'd felt earlier. 'You say you're not in a relationship so who is Bill? And don't lie to me—I know he lives with you because Joe told me as much the first day we met, when he was hurt.'

He'd expected embarrassment so was surprised when Lauren laughed, the sound so joyous and whole-hearted his anger spiked, then faded, because Lauren laughing was a beautiful sight.

'Oh, Jean-Luc, I'm sorry,' she eventually spluttered, 'but I was picturing me with Bill. Bill's a darling and I love him dearly, but he's Russ's partner, not mine. From the time we realised I was pregnant, Joe became a family concern. Russ and Bill took over, pointing out that I still needed to finish my education and that we'd need some kind of community living arrangement so there'd always be someone there for the baby. Bill had been offered a job back in Sydney so he and Russ returned and, through the hospital, got the house, which is divided into three flats. I wanted to be independent, and I needed to work, but I didn't want to put Joe into child-care, so all of us living in the same building made things easy.'

Jean-Luc made a noise that must have signified under-standing, because Lauren continued.

'Russ played cricket for the state and Bill's a soccer player and they're both mad on sport so they took on all the sports stuff, and Mum's been the chief babysitter except when she's busy preparing for an exhibition—she's a painter. Then we have a wonderful nanny who comes in— or we did when Joe was little.'

'I'm sorry, but I hate them all,' Jean-Luc declared. 'And you should have turned left back there—you've gone too far and will have to go back.'

Lauren drove on to the next intersection and turned back, only half her mind on the road and traffic.

'You hate them all?' she echoed, and Jean-Luc sighed.

'Sour grapes!' he said. 'Pure envy! That is *my* child's history you're talking about—it was I who should have taught him soccer. As for cricket, pah, it is a sissy game!'

Lauren wanted to laugh again but she'd heard a note of real hurt in Jean-Luc's voice and that hurt cut into her, as sharp as a blade.

'I'm sorry, it was foolish of me to talk to you that way,' she said, pulling into the side street he'd indicated. She stopped the car and turned to look at him. 'Do you really feel so strongly about what you've missed?'

He stared at her, his blue eyes dark with disbelief.

'How could I not?' he demanded, then he sighed again. 'And here I go, getting angry with you again, when I know you are not to blame. It was some malign fate that did this to us, but to lose so much of my son's life, how could I not be angry?'

Lauren couldn't answer—there was no answer—and right now they had a job to do.

She located the house number Katie had given her and parked outside, the front door of the little white house opening as she got out of the car.

'Are you Katie's friend?' the motherly-looking woman asked, then she frowned as Jean-Luc also left the car. 'Is something wrong with Katie—is that why there are two of you?'

Lauren hurried forward, speaking reassuringly, and an hour later, after tea and scones, baked in honour of the visitors and covered with lashings of home-made jam and cream, Lauren and Jean-Luc departed. Mrs Malone was already packing a bag to take to Sydney where she'd stay with her sister close to the hospital and provide all the support Katie and Brooke would need.

'Well,' Jean-Luc said as they drove away, 'that is one happy woman.'

Lauren nodded, remembering that it was her talk with Katie and mention of Mrs Malone that had pushed her into telling Jean-Luc about Joe.

Had that been a good thing?

She wasn't sure because apart from being angry over missing out on Joe's early childhood she still didn't know where the three of them stood. Not that Jean-Luc had had time to sort out things like a long-term connection…

'You said the lifesavers—you would show me them at work.'

His prompt made her realise she was sitting behind the wheel of the car, staring into space.

'Of course,' she said, and started the engine, reasonably sure this road would lead them to the beach and that some-where by the beach she'd find the lifesavers' clubhouse. It was summer, there would be someone on patrol, and it would be an excuse to get out of the car, which seemed to be getting smaller and smaller so every move Jean-Luc made registered on her skin and tingled along her nerves.

Down at the beach she found a parking place right outside the clubhouse.

'Lifesavers work voluntarily,' she explained. 'They are mostly teenagers but some members stay on so you get life-savers of all ages. They have rostered times they do patrols, and these days have jet-skis and rubber duckies—rubber boats—they can use to go out to rescue people.'

They got out of the car and walked around the building,

Jean-Luc smelling the tang of the ocean and feeling more at peace than he had since coming to Australia—certainly since he'd run into Lauren again.

Although the fact that he was here with her was definitely adding to his sense of well-being, and that was odd.

Ominous!

He didn't need a woman to complete his life, so why would he feel that way?

But she was talking again, about red and yellow flags and why people had to stay between them because of rips and currents and because that was the safe area the lifesavers—who mostly looked about fifteen—could patrol.

He listened and took it in, but in another part of his mind he was already walking on that beach—on the soft white sand that beckoned so invitingly. Far out there a few surfers rode their boards, legs dangling over the sides, waiting for a wave, but if lifesavers were on watch this late in the afternoon, there were few people in the surf for them to stand guard over. Maybe six or seven further up the beach.

But the urge to plunge into the green waves that broke against the shore was growing stronger. His underwear was most respectable—far more modest than the tiny bathing costumes some of the men on the beach were wearing.

'We can have a swim?'

Caught halfway through an explanation of a surf rescue, Lauren looked startled and probably should have been put out but instead she smiled—a radiant smile of such sheer delight it brought back the weird feeling Jean-Luc had suffered the night before.

The one that wasn't lust...

'I'd love one,' Lauren said. 'I have gear in the car. There's almost sure to be a pair of shorts of Bill's or Russ's if you want. I know there are towels. I'll just get them. There are changing rooms at the back of the club. Oh, a swim will be lovely!'

She disappeared back to the car and Jean-Luc watched her go. What was he doing, going swimming with this woman? Seeing her fully clad sent his libido into overdrive, so in a swimming costume?

And what had happened to his careful, ordered life?

D'accord! So finding out about Joe had been a shock, but he had to think that through—divorce himself from the emotion he'd stupidly felt—and consider the situation rationally. Working out what happened next was an intellectual exercise, not an emotional one. Emotions only muddied clear thinking.

Lauren was back, holding up a pair of long shorts, bright blue with white hibiscus flowers all over them. Very large hibiscus flowers.

She must have read his horror, for she laughed and said, 'If your underwear is respectable, you can swim in that—people do, all the time. But you could try the shorts then you won't have to drive back to Sydney in wet underwear, or commando if that's what you'd prefer.'

She grinned at him and disappeared, presumably to change, leaving him with the bright shorts.

Oh, well, there would be no one he knew on this beach in far-off Australia, so maybe he *could* wear them. He found his way to the changing rooms and came out to find Lauren not waiting for him but already striding across the sand towards the water.

He'd have known her body anywhere. It may have been ten years but that figure in the black one-piece was not very different to the twenty-one-year-old who'd also walked ahead of him, innumerable times, on another beach, far, far away. Even at twenty-one she'd had the curves of a much more mature woman, the swell of hips below her waist, the tightly rounded buttocks, and when she turned, lush breasts, deep and full.

He was glad he was wearing the extremely roomy board shorts as his body was behaving even more badly than it had in the car. And not that he'd seen her breasts in the swimming costume. Not until she'd found a bare patch of sand on which to drop her towels and clothes did she turn to see if he was coming.

Yes, breasts still just as full, a deep cleft not visible from where he was but very vivid in his memory. And suddenly he ached with the pain of wanting her, yet knew this was wrong—it wasn't her he wanted at all, but the young Lauren whom he'd loved.

Or was it?

He no longer knew, although this Lauren wasn't so different—giving up a day off to sit with a single mother while her baby had an operation. Driving down here to find some support for that young mother. Caring, generous, selfless and giving, the young Lauren had been all those things and he suspected she was just the same at thirty-one.

And beautiful!

So why had she not married?

The puzzle was simmering in his brain as he reached her, and in an effort to distract himself from the tug of her physical beauty he asked.

'Have you never married? Never thought of marrying?'

She shook her head and the dark hair, streaked with rich red in the sun, swirled and tossed in the sea breeze.

'Not many men are interested in a woman who has a child, especially when that child has a disability.'

'But some men would have accepted Joe as part of the package,' he argued, seeing her beauty stripped almost bare in front of him and knowing how attractive she would be to men of any age.

She studied him for a moment, then she sighed.

'I didn't just want marriage, Jean-Luc,' she said quietly. 'This might sound foolish, but somewhere deep inside me I knew I'd already experienced love and I didn't want to denigrate that love by accepting some kind of compromise. And the relationships I had felt like that—like compromise.'

He shook his head.

'That is exactly the kind of thing my Lauren would have said. Honest as the day was long, my Lauren.'

Her eyes darkened and she frowned slightly, and he wondered what he'd said to upset her. Then she shook her head and was about to walk away, down to the water, when he stopped her with a touch on her arm.

'What is it?' he asked quietly.

Still she hesitated, then finally a small, embarrassed smile chased across her lips.

'Do you think that way?' she asked. 'Think of that Lauren as someone else? Not me at all?'

He knew this was important to her so he searched for how to put it, but in the end what could he tell her but the truth?

'I *knew* that Lauren,' he explained. 'Knew you as you were ten years ago. But you must know how much you've changed—how you've grown and matured. You've studied, worked, had a child and had to conquer all the hassles of his early upbringing, to say nothing of the challenges of his disability. You have become independent, for all your family are close by, so you can run your own life. You aren't my Lauren any more than I am the same man you fell in love with at St Catherine's. I'm a stranger to you because you have no memory of me, but you are no less a stranger to me.'

She studied him for a moment longer then nodded her head, accepting what he'd said but obviously still thinking about it.

Finally she smiled, a broad, joyous grin.

'Well, at least we're both strangers,' she said. 'Race you to the water!'

And across the years he heard the echo of that cry, so as he followed her—she'd always started first—he wasn't sure just how true the words he'd spoken really were.

The water was so invitingly cool he dived beneath the waves, then joined her as she surfed back to shore, catching her ankle as she tried to stand in the shallows where the waves had deposited them.

She fell across him, laughing, her wet hair tangled across her face so he raised his hand to lift a strand free of her mouth.

Free of her lips, now slightly parted as she regained her breath, but this was not Lauren of the past, or a stranger—this was a woman to whom he was infinitely attracted and who, he suspected, was in turn attracted to him.

He still held her ankle in one hand and he tugged on it so she slid through the shallows until she was lying in the water right beside him, hair now splaying out, floating on the surface.

'Mermaid's hair,' he whispered, and ran his hand across it to smooth it out. 'Mermaid's lips, pink-red and inviting. Is kissing on a beach permitted or will the lifesavers come after us and throw us into jail?'

And once again she didn't answer straight away, her gaze roaming his face as if to read some answers to unspoken questions.

'Kissing is OK,' she finally said, and if she sounded breathless, well, that was all right, his chest was feeling kind of tight as well.

He half floated beside her, one hand on the sand, anchoring him, the other resting on her shoulder. Then he touched his lips to hers, a suggestion of a kiss, knowing this was Lauren now, not Lauren then, and they were starting a whole new voyage of discovery.

Nibbling kisses, lips and bodies touching and moving apart, both of them still at the mercy of the waves, sometimes floating, sometimes on the sand or half-afloat, depending on the depth of water washing in and out.

But even as he was kissing Lauren—and enjoying it— he knew it was a diversion. While he was kissing Lauren he didn't have to think—didn't have to consider the implications of the child he'd fathered but didn't know, or where the future might lead as far as that child was concerned.

How could he possibly be a father to a child who lived thousands of miles away?

Did he want to be involved?

A clenching of his gut told him the question was ridiculous. How could he not want involvement?

'Hey, you're going to drown me.'

Lauren eased away from under his body, which seemed to have floated over hers while he was distracted. And he must have looked distracted because she smiled and said lightly, 'Is kissing in the shallows such a worry?'

'I was thinking about Joe.'

She sat up in the shallow water, her wet hair tangled

around her head, sand showing in the black strands, but the hazel eyes that met his held no indication that she cared about her appearance—sand in her hair the least of her worries.

'I've thought of nothing else since last night—not of Joe, but of how you must feel and what you might want to do,' she said, and she reached out and took his hand, as a friend might, offering comfort or support. 'You need to get to know him a little at least before you can make any decisions, and he doesn't need to be lumped with a father just like that, so I thought…'

Her eyes looked anxious and he realised she hadn't changed very much at all, still worrying about other people and trying to do what was best for them. He lifted the hand that held his to his lips and pressed a kiss on the back of it.

'You thought…' he prompted, his heart suddenly thudding in his chest, but whether because he was holding Lauren's hand or because he was uncertain what she was about to say, he didn't know.

'I thought, when you had time, you might do things with us.'

She tried to tug her hand away and he could see pinkness in her cheeks as if the kiss—or her suggestion?—had embarrassed her. But he held onto it, even kissed it again.

And because he didn't answer she rushed to fill the silence that was growing thicker by the second.

'He's already disposed to like you—he calls you John, which is probably the best he can manage with Jean-Luc.'

'He talks about me?'

Jean-Luc was sufficiently distracted by this information to allow Lauren to retrieve her hand and now with it safely out of kissing distance she smiled at him.

'You *did* buy twenty pairs of socks,' she reminded him.

'Such munificence looms large in a young mind. He tells everyone about his friend John.'

'So, what kind of expeditions did you have in mind?'

And although she'd sounded so confident when she'd made the first suggestion, Jean-Luc sensed a hesitation in her now.

Because of Joe, or for herself?

'Well, we walk Lucy in the park most days and next week there's an open day at Joe's school, and Saturday morning is Nippers—you can come along and sit on the beach and see what Nippers do—then in a couple of weeks the Cub group is running a sausage sizzle at the local hardware store—that's a Saturday morning. All this would depend on when you're available and also how much you want to do…'

How much did he want to do?

Lauren's suggestion was excellent, all the suggestions she'd made would be natural ways for him to ease himself into Joe's life, but that was for now.

The future beyond now yawned like a deep black hole.

And what about Lauren's life?

Would he be easing himself into it at the same time?

Did he want that?

Did she?

'It was easier when we were kissing,' he said, as a bigger wave tumbled her closer and he caught her in his arms—a tall, shapely, vibrant woman. Why *wouldn't* his body respond?

They left the water eventually and walked up the beach, Lauren reaching the towels first, lifting one and handing it to him, then lifting her own and shaking the sand off it.

And as she shook it the car keys fell out, and he bent to

THE HEART SURGEON'S SECRET CHILD

pick them up for her. A small bunch, no doubt just the car key and door keys for the house and flat, but what caught his attention was the silver heart attached to the keyring. He stared at it, then rubbed his forefinger around it, tracing the shape of the heart, for that was all it was, a heart-shaped piece of metal, probably not silver at all.

'I gave you this,' he said, still staring at the object, unable to believe how strongly the past had come rushing over him.

'This is how my heart will be—empty—when we part,' he'd said.

Lauren turned to face him, a puzzled frown on her face. 'My car keys?'

'This heart—or one very like it. I bought it at the silversmith's in the village near St Catherine's and he didn't have a chain so you wore it on a leather thong around your neck.'

'Oh, Jean-Luc,' she whispered, wonder thickening her voice. 'It's all I had when they found me. My clothes were in tatters but this heart was around my neck. Apparently someone tried to take it off, thinking it might choke me if I had a seizure, but I refused to let anyone touch it. Then, when I got home, I didn't want to wear it because people kept asking me where I'd got it and I didn't know, but I wanted it with me anyway.'

He took her in his arms and kissed her once again, kissed her as he'd kissed her when he'd hung the heart around her neck—when they'd both been young, and loving had been easy and uncomplicated...

CHAPTER SEVEN

'SO, TELL me why a male dog is called Lucy?'

Without doubt her suggestion that Jean-Luc spend time with Joe was the worst idea Lauren had ever had. The man had become a constant presence in her life—at work, forever in the PICU, checking the babies, chatting to parents, his accented voice sending shivers down her spine and reminders of his kisses deep into her belly.

Now here they were in the park, Joe throwing sticks for Lucy while Jean-Luc sat, far too close to her, on the seat beside the ornamental lake.

'He's a failed seeing-eye dog,' Lauren replied, glad to have something to talk about, though talking did little to distract her body from its pathetic behaviour—heating up, shivering, producing tremors when he accidentally touched her—whenever Jean-Luc was around.

'A failed seeing-eye dog?'

Her companion sounded so incredulous she had to smile and now she turned to face him, although looking at those blue eyes and the scars on his cheeks made her want to touch him so sitting on her hands seemed the only option.

'He was born in the kennels of the Blind Association but when it came to doing the final training, he didn't make it.

These dogs are still really well trained so they are often offered to people with disabilities as companion dogs. Russ called him Lucifer—the fallen angel—but of course that soon became Lucy. But he's trained to alert us if Joe gets into trouble—if he should faint or fall and hurt himself. Some dogs are trained to respond to changes in their human's chemical make-up so they know when their human is going to have an epileptic fit, for example.'

'I have heard of these dogs, but Joe, there is danger of him fainting? You, or someone, spoke of a heart condition—was his problem fixed?'

'He was born with a ventricular septal defect, but it was small and seems to have closed itself. There's still a slight murmur but not enough to put him through an operation, or so Alex says and I agree.'

She stopped suddenly as she realised the import of what she'd just said.

'I'm sorry, that sounded very—I don't know, possessive, I suppose. But I've been the one making decisions about his health all this time. I can show you his health records, what I have of them, and as a heart specialist yourself— I don't know, Jean-Luc, this is so difficult.'

He took her hand and all the physical symptoms of her attraction she'd managed to ignore while she'd talked of Joe came raging back to life.

'I want to be his father, not his doctor, and I am sure whatever you and Alex decided was correct. Don't blame yourself, Lauren, or get caught up in guilt. Neither of us intended to be in this situation, and we're both confused about the path that lies ahead of us, so tell me more about Lucy, or talk of other things. Tomorrow we go to Nippers? Do we go to Coogee? Is that where he belongs?'

Lauren looked at her hand, tanned against Jean-Luc's paler and larger one, and wondered how she'd landed herself in this situation. For sure, she'd always wanted to find Joe's father, but she hadn't intended falling in love with him. Yet that *had* to be what was happening, had to be why her heart turned over when she saw him and her skin heated when he was close to her and she felt weak-kneed when she saw him pick up a baby. That was more than physical attraction surely.

And as she didn't remember the man she'd known before, she had to accept it was this man she loved—this virtual stranger.

'Yes, it's Coogee,' she said, sounding very calm for someone who had just suffered a revelation of gigantic proportions. 'And it's early. We need to be at the beach at seven so I'll pick you up at six-thirty—that's if you really want to go.'

Blue eyes scanned her face—please, heaven, he couldn't see her thoughts—then he smiled and said, 'Try to stop me!'

Her heart did its leaping, somersaulting act and it wasn't the smile that had caused it but the genuine interest he was showing in Joe.

Although, if he grew too interested, might he not want Joe in his life full time?

He lived in France—thousands of miles away.

Joe's home was here.

With her.

Jean-Luc put his arm along the back of the seat, so his hand was resting just above her shoulder. It was distracting but not so distracting she wasn't watching what was going on with Joe and Lucy. Now Joe threw the stick into the water this time, and Lucy plunged in after it, Joe following.

'Brat of a child!' Lauren said, forgetting distraction and rushing towards the shallow lake. 'You know not to go into the water in your sneakers,' she scolded, catching Joe's arm and hauling him to the shore. 'And now Lucy is all wet and the water is smelly. Who's going to wash her?'

'John will,' Joe announced, beaming at Jean-Luc who had rapidly become a special champion in his eyes.

'John wash Lucy?' he asked, his voice telling them he was confident of agreement.

Lauren turned to see how Jean-Luc would take this request and to her surprise the Frenchman seemed unfazed.

'Lead me to the tap, Joe,' he said, and so they all walked home together, where Lauren stood back and watched all three of them get very, very wet, laughing and joking, the hose turning onto Joe and Jean-Luc as well as Lucy, the laughter and delight in her son's eyes actually hurting her heart.

Yes, Joe had had family all around him from his birth, but he hadn't had a father…

And her heart kept hurting. It hurt as she and Jean-Luc sat on the beach and watched Joe in Nippers beach races, and when she saw the French surgeon cooking sausages outside the hardware store. Jean-Luc was getting to know his son, and Joe clearly adored the man, but they were no further advanced as far as the future was concerned.

'You have to talk to him, ask him if he's given any thought to what he wants to do,' Lauren's mother urged, three weeks after the afternoon at Thirroul beach, when it seemed that Jean-Luc had become a fixture in their extended family. He went sailing on the harbour with Russ and Bill, exchanged recipes for bouillabaisse with her mother, took Joe to Cubs in Lauren's little car and generally spent most of his off-duty hours with Joe.

Joe, not her!

True, he'd asked her out to dinner a couple of times—to talk about Joe, of course—but one evening she'd promised to go to a hens' party for Becky and the next time she'd had a long-standing arrangement to catch up with a friend from nursing school.

So that was that. He hadn't asked again and as far as she could make out, she wasn't part of the situation that was Joe—well, not at the moment.

And to be fair, Jean-Luc was working a lot of late shifts so he could see more of Joe during the day…

Or he didn't want to ask her out.

'Will you be there when they do the operation?'

Lauren shook away her wandering thoughts, chastising herself for letting them wander at work. The anaesthetist had given Jeremy Willis the pre-med for his operation and Lauren was watching him to make sure it worked, leaving him suitably drowsy.

'I'm not usually, because they usually do catheterisations in the cath lab and it's too small for onlookers, but as it's in theatre, I suppose I could go in, if that would make you feel easier.'

Rosemary hugged her.

'It really would, if you wouldn't mind. I'd go in myself only I'd faint for sure, but if you're there, I'll feel so much better. I know you have Jeremy's interests at heart. I know the doctors are good and all that, but to them he's just another case.'

Lauren started to protest, but Rosemary was in full flow.

'And that French doctor, the one who'll do the operation—does he really have children of his own?'

Oops! Jean-Luc certainly hadn't known about Joe when he'd made his statement to Rosemary.

But now?

'He has a son,' Lauren said, glad she was able to answer honestly.

'Oh, that's good. And is his wife out in Australia with him?'

The question was so obvious Lauren thought back to the first time she'd met Rosemary Willis. Had there been a Mr Willis present? And even if there had been, did it mean they were still married?

'I don't know,' she answered honestly, and suddenly the enormity of what she'd said struck her like a physical blow. She'd been so caught up in sorting out Jean-Luc and Joe she'd forgotten all about Jean-Luc's private life.

In fact, perhaps because he was here on his own for six months, she'd just assumed he wasn't married, but why wouldn't he be? The two point four children she'd originally imagined were probably at school and six months in a foreign country would prove too disruptive.

But he'd kissed her.

'Ah, Mrs Willis! How are you today?'

The man who'd suddenly cast Lauren's thoughts into total confusion eased into the room.

'Sister!' he said politely, nodding at Lauren as if she were a casual acquaintance, not someone who'd cooked damper for him the previous evening.

Not that cooking damper was an intimate kind of thing, especially with Joe helping.

'Jeremy prepped?'

Lauren thrust all extraneous thoughts from her mind and turned to meet the blue eyes she now knew so well.

'The anaesthetist has just left, she said she'd meet you in theatre.'

'Good.'

Jean-Luc moved closer to the bed, and took Jeremy's hand.

'You know we're going to fix that bothersome hole of yours,' he said gently. 'You'll go to sleep and when you wake up you'll still feel tired, but in a day or two you'll be running around and not getting breathless at all. Is that good for you?'

Jeremy nodded sleepily, and Jean-Luc left the room, Rosemary following him out, asking questions that Lauren felt weren't really relevant.

Or was that just bitchiness?

The thought surprised her. If asked to honestly describe herself she wouldn't have included bitchy as one of her negative qualities.

But there was no time to take the thought further for the orderlies arrived to take Jeremy to theatre where the procedure would be done so as many of the team as possible could watch.

Inside the theatre Lauren stayed well back from the operating table, but extra screens had been set up so the people not close to the main screen of the echocardiogram and ultrasound machines could see what was happening and follow the path of the catheter up the vein and into the heart, where the tiny occluder would be put into position to close the hole.

She watched, enthralled, although she'd often seen cardiac catheterisations done, as the tiny wire threaded its way towards Jeremy's heart. Maggie was reciting pulse and blood-pressure readings, oxygen levels, letting Jean-Luc know the child was doing well, so the alarm, when it came, shocked everyone. A loud beep and one glance at the monitor above the operating table told the story—Jeremy's heart had stopped beating.

Jean-Luc reacted first, ordering drugs from Maggie, his voice crisp, not panicked. Alex, standing near the head of the table, hit Jeremy's chest with his fist, hoping to shock the heart back to life. Nothing changed and Alex began cardiac massage, pushing down on the small chest, counting. Maggie had administered the drugs, while Jean-Luc withdrew the catheter, as yet only part way towards the heart.

'Some kind of insult? A chemical imbalance? Damn, we tested him and tested him, he was right to go!' Alex muttered, while Phil asked the question no one wanted to hear. Did they open Jeremy's chest and manually get his heart beating?

Alex made the decision and the cut, but less than an hour later they had to admit that they'd lost their little patient.

Lauren slumped against the wall, totally exhausted as the tension that had held her immobile during all the drama slowly drained away.

'I'll go and speak to Mrs Willis,' Alex said.

'And I,' Jean-Luc offered, his voice hoarse with emotion, his face so white his scars stood out like whip marks against his skin.

He was shattered. Lauren could see it in the way he breathed—slowly and carefully, as if each inhalation hurt—and the way he walked, back straight and chest up, trying to minimise his limp, but more like an automaton than a human being.

And his pain transferred itself to her—as if she needed

more for she, too, must speak to Rosemary Willis. But that, she realised, must be the price you paid for love— feeling someone else's pain so intensely.

The day dragged on, emotional scene after emotional scene, discussions and investigations, the mood in the PICU so strained Lauren was relieved to finally go off duty.

But once Joe was settled into bed she knew she had to see Jean-Luc, the thought of him bearing his sadness all alone too much for her to think about.

He didn't answer when she pressed the bell for his flat but she wasn't going to be put off. She pressed the bell for Grace's flat and gave a little wave to the security camera so Grace could see it was her.

The door clicked open and Lauren walked into the lobby, looking up as Grace came down the stairs.

'He's in his flat,' she said, when Lauren explained she wanted to see Jean-Luc. 'I've tried to talk to him but he, very politely, told me to mind my own business. He never locks his front door if you want to go in.'

Lauren hesitated and Grace gave her an exasperated look.

'Go on in,' she said. 'He needs someone!'

Lauren tapped on the door, then called Jean-Luc's name as she entered the flat, glancing first into the living room.

He was sitting by the window.

'I saw you come,' he said, his voice devoid of all emotion, his head still half-turned towards the window. 'One more person ready to tell me it wasn't my fault!'

The goad was just what Lauren needed to get her over the threshold. She stepped into the room, anger settling where sympathy had been earlier.

'Of course I'm not going to tell you that—you're an intelligent man, a specialist. If you don't know that then you shouldn't be doing the job you're doing.'

He turned to face her and she saw the ravished agony on his face and stepped closer, drawn to him—wanting to do something, anything, to ease his pain.

'Actually,' she said, trying for a smile but aware it was probably a terrible effort as she was feeling decidedly shaky, 'I came to give you a hug. I figured even if you are married and somehow we've never got around to discussing that, but if you were, given you are here so far from home, no wife would object to you getting a hug from an old friend in these circumstances.'

Now she was standing right beside him and she could see a slight smile curling his lips. It made her uneasy, that smile. Not a particularly nice smile.

'Did you think about the wife back home the times we've kissed?' he asked, confirming the not-niceness of the smile.

But she guessed this was his way of pushing her away—of not accepting her offer of sympathy—so she persevered.

'No, but in retrospect you were kissing the old Lauren then,' she reminded him. 'The one you kissed before you were married so I think that's kind of all right, but before the hug, and you're getting it no matter how hard you try to put me off, perhaps we could establish the marriage thing.'

He sighed then he stood up and put his arms around her, tucking her close to his body.

'You're right. I probably do need a hug—some human contact to remind me life goes on. And, no, sweet Lauren, I am not married, although once I was.'

She felt put out, although why on earth she should have expected him to remain true to some young girl with whom he'd spent six weeks she didn't know. But the peevish feeling didn't last long as standing like this, so close to Jean-Luc's body, was igniting all the fires of attraction.

She put her arms around him and hugged him hard.

'It was terrible, but babies die, Jean-Luc, children die. You and Alex and all the surgeons like you can only do so much. I know you know that, and that me saying it won't make the shock and pain of losing that little boy go away, but I don't have anything else to offer—just words and a hug.'

He said nothing, but his arms tightened around her and they stood together in the dim room, lit only by a street-light on the footpath outside the house.

Then the hug changed. Jean-Luc's body shifted, and he moved his head so he could look into Lauren's face.

'Just so you know, this is not the old Lauren I'm about to kiss,' he said, then his lips met hers, and he caught her gasp in his mouth as his body, hard and hot, pressed against hers.

And as his lips seared hers she tried to think—had the beach kisses been like this?—then her mind gave up to sen-sation and she was swamped with a feverish desire. And as Jean-Luc's hands began a slow and tantalising explora-tion of her body, sliding down to cup her buttocks and pull her closer, so her own hands explored, her fingers seeking his head, threading into his hair, holding his head to hers so the kiss would never end.

But end it did and she gave a little moan of regret that turned to another gasp, for now he was kissing her neck and the hollow in her shoulder, his tongue teasing at her skin, his warm breath adding fuel to the flames already licking through her body.

His hands brushed across her breasts and she gasped again, this time against his ear, where she'd been nibbling at a lobe.

Someone was moaning now and she was pretty sure it

wasn't Jean-Luc, but as she pressed her body harder against his, feeling his arousal, hot and taut against her stomach, Jean-Luc moved, lifting her into his arms and striding through to his bedroom to toss her onto the bed.

He knelt beside her, then eased one knee across her lower body so he was astride her without resting his weight on her body.

'Let us get some things straight,' he said, 'before we proceed.'

He sounded so formal Lauren would have smiled, only she was too confused, her body longing for his touch, for whatever he could give her, while her mind—well, it had gone AWOL as far as she could tell. She was unable to think at all—or think of anything other than sex right now!

'This is not a pity—I do not know a word that isn't rude—but you know what I mean. If we make love now, it is not because you are sorry for me, *non*?'

Lauren nodded, then wondered if that was the right response. Apparently it was, for her about-to-be lover continued in the same strained voice.

'And you are Lauren, my colleague and, I think, my friend, not the ghost of the past—*d'accord*?'

Another nod—Jean-Luc said '*d'accord*' so often she'd looked it up in her recently acquired French-English dictionary and found out it was used much the same as she used the word 'OK.'

'And we will not be having another mistake like Joe for although he is a delightful child, he *was* a mistake—we took precautions back then, although you don't remember, but maybe the condoms I bought in India were not reliable. But condoms I have now because I am a man and I will be responsible for you.'

Did she have to nod again? She'd never had a conversation about condoms with a would-be lover before—well, not that she could remember—so she didn't know how to react, and before she could decide he was talking again.

'And you should also know that making love is not a prelude to marriage. I have, in your English saying, been there and done that. It didn't work for me but as well as that, we do not know each other well, not yet, not the people we are now, so marriage might not suit us.'

First condoms now this! Lauren had had enough!

'Oh, for heaven's sake, Jean-Luc, are we going to have sex or are you going to keep talking all night? I know I haven't had a lot of experience but I'm damned sure most people don't go through all this ridiculous preamble. We have a child between us, and that hasn't been sorted out but, believe me, I'm not about to go rushing into marriage with you or anyone else, thank you very much! Marrying you is the very last thing on my mind—particularly right now!'

He looked so shocked Lauren had to laugh, then she reached out and drew his head towards her and kissed him gently on the lips.

'I'm all grown up now—I understand about attraction and sex. In fact, Jasmine keeps telling me it will make my skin glow so, please, can we keep going?'

And now he smiled and she realised most of his talk had been nerves, as most of her head-nodding had been.

'Then we should see if we can make your skin glow,' he said softly.

He moved so he could kiss her again, this time on the inside of her arm, the last part of her body she would have imagined would be an erogenous zone. But the feelings he was generating were definitely erotic, and as his lips moved up her arm, then across to her breasts, covered well in bra and T-shirt, she shivered, realising that what was about to happen would be like making love for the very first time.

Excitement grew within her, charging through her body so her fingers trembled as she helped Jean-Luc remove her clothing, and shook even worse as she helped him with his.

Was this how it was before between them? She wanted to ask but knew asking would take them out of the magic that was now, but with every move she wondered if maybe this would trigger her memory and the blank six weeks would finally return.

'Oh!' she whispered quietly as once again his lips took possession of her breast, but at the same time his hand was exploring further down, brushing across her nest of wiry hair, delving into the moist lips, touching and withdrawing, teasing her until she shuddered with what could only be desire, but desire for what? How would it feel?

Now he kissed her inner thigh, his hand on her breast, his lips chasing where his fingers had been, in the intimate centre of her body. And as his tongue brushed against the most sensitive of places she gasped aloud then grabbed his head and held him there, although calling to him to stop, and then again to go on, while all the time tension built and built in her body, until with one brush of his tongue and a hard touch on her nipples her world exploded, her cries only muffled by the fist she thrust into her mouth—biting on her fingers as shame that Grace might hear came bearing down on her.

Then Jean-Luc was beside her, a smile on his face, his hard, insistent penis brushing against her moist opening.

'Guide me in,' he whispered, and without thought she did just that, touching and feeling him, lifting her hips and moving her body so he slid inside the warm wet sheath. Then together they moved. Was this remembered movement or something bred into a woman? She tried again to think but the tension she'd felt earlier was building again—a good tension, not a bad one—hard and tight and desperate until once again she burst apart, pins and needles rushing through her body, tingling in her toes.

'My toes tingled,' she said in wonder, as Jean-Luc, with a final gasp, collapsed on top of her.

She held his body, held him tight, enjoying the weight of him, the heat, the smooth, satiny feel of his skin, the smell of sex and man.

'Your toes tingled ten years ago,' he said against her neck, pressing little kisses there, not hot kisses, just friendly, gentle ones—like the hug she'd come to give him.

'I wish I could remember,' she whispered as he lifted his body off hers, but kept his arms around her so they lay side by side, legs entangled, bodies touching, heads far enough apart for them to look into each other's eyes.

'Maybe you will eventually,' he said, and suddenly Lauren was sorry she'd brought up the past. Jean-Luc was right—this was now.

But where would now lead?

Not to marriage, he'd made that clear. And she'd been honest when she'd said marriage was the last thing on her mind.

Yet…

'Why didn't your marriage work out?' she asked, the intimacy they'd just shared making the question seem OK.

She heard him sigh, then he reached out and stroked the hair away from her face.

'It was probably my fault in that I was too involved in

my work. We had been childhood sweethearts and drifted into marriage too early. So!' He paused and for a while she wondered if he would add more. Wondered what he was thinking about. Then finally he said, very quietly, 'My work—it has been enough.'

Not it *is* enough, Lauren thought, but she didn't say it, too saddened to think that Jean-Luc, who could show such joyousness when playing with Joe and Lucy, had locked away that part of him, and hidden in his work.

Not her business—he'd made that very plain…

CHAPTER EIGHT

LAUREN returned to work, hopefully not glowing, but the mood in the unit remained subdued. The autopsy had found no reason why Jeremy's heart had stopped beating and although the specialists were still awaiting the results of toxicology tests, he had not been given any drugs that hadn't been used on him before, so his death remained a mystery.

And a burden on the hearts of all who had known the little boy, or been involved in the operation. Lauren knew Jean-Luc was the most affected, so she wasn't particularly worried to see him having lunch in the canteen with Rosemary Willis a couple of days after Jeremy's death.

She herself had not seen much of Jean-Luc since that momentous night so she felt a little put out. But tonight was Cubs' night and it had become his habit to collect Joe from the house, and drive him to his meeting, then wait and bring him back, joining the family for a late dinner.

She waited for him, tense and anxious, embarrassed as well, not sure how to meet and greet a new lover. Or were they lovers? Had it been nothing more than a one-night stand—a hug taken to the next step?

No, he'd denied it was that!

When he didn't turn up she drove Joe to Cubs herself,

telling him Jean-Luc was busy at the hospital, but her return trip took her past Scoozi's and even if she hadn't seen the tall dark-haired man with the slight hesitation in his stride, Joe, of course, wouldn't miss him.

'There's John,' he shrieked. 'Let's stop and talk to him. Tell him all I did at Cubs tonight.'

Lauren took one look at the woman by Jean-Luc's side—Rosemary Willis in a very small little black dress—and kept driving.

'Let's not,' she said, trying to swallow the bitterness in her mouth—telling herself the woman had just lost a child and needed whatever support she could get.

He knocked on the door the next evening.

'Is Joe still up? I wanted to apologise for missing Cubs. I had an important meeting.'

With Rosemary Willis? Lauren wanted to say, but didn't, ashamed that she could feel so jealous.

'Well, can I come in?'

And something in his voice made Lauren really look at him, study him with eyes stripped of her own emotions. He looked grey and tired, far worse than he had the day Jeremy had died, and she opened the door wider and stepped away so he could pass by her.

Except that he didn't. He stopped beside her and touched her gently on the shoulder.

'I have neglected you as well—but I did not wish to push my demons onto you, Lauren. I must deal with them myself.'

'Why?'

The question came out far too bluntly, but she, of all people, knew about demons.

He half smiled at her.

'Because they are mental. These demons are inside my head—and only I can exorcise them.'

'That's probably because you haven't tried any other way,' she said. 'Because you think, man-like, that you should be able to overcome all the obstacles in the world just through your own intelligence and persistence and strength, and if all else fails a bit of duct tape. Man stuff. And because you're a man you won't ask for help or even accept it when it's offered. You need to talk about your feelings, Jean-Luc, not keep them all bottled up inside you. OK, so talking might not provide an answer but it's a release valve—believe me, I know. As you said the other night, I've been there and done that!'

He looked at her, really looked at her, and she knew she'd snagged his attention.

'You had demons? After the accident?'

She had to smile.

'Didn't you?' she said softly, touching his hand and feeling relief flood through her when his fingers turned to grip hers in a tight hold.

'I did, but mine were mostly vanity, though at the time I couldn't see that, but you, with no memory—how did that affect you?'

'Got all night?' Lauren joked, and then realised what she'd said and blushed. 'I meant to talk,' she amended hurriedly, but Jean-Luc had tugged her closer so their bodies were almost touching.

'I have all night for you,' he said quietly. 'For talk or whatever else you want.'

She stared at him.

This wasn't right.

He'd wound her round his little finger once again and

here she was mentally packing a toothbrush and heading for his house to spend the night.

And last night he'd been out with Rosemary Willis and though she hadn't watched all night, she was reasonably certain he hadn't come home early…

'But first I must see Joe.'

The reminder of why Jean-Luc had come broke through Lauren's wild imaginings.

Joe was sitting at the kitchen table, painstakingly writing names on envelopes, Lucy under the table at his feet.

As Jean-Luc came in, Lucy eased out from under the table and though she wagged her tail in greeting, she gave a low growl as well.

Come near my charge at your peril.

Lauren had printed the names of his friends in large letters on a sheet of paper and Joe was copying them. He looked up when Jean-Luc came in and beamed with delight.

'You come to my birthday party, John?' he asked, waving an invitation with a picture of a clown and balloons. 'We're having cake.'

'I'd love to come,' Jean-Luc replied. 'When is it?'

'Saturday.'

Satisfied he had another guest, Joe returned to his laborious task.

'It's Saturday week, in fact,' Lauren said. 'Though Joe's getting so excited he'll probably be over it by then. We only have a party for him every second year. The in-between year we go to the zoo, or Underwater World, or somewhere special.'

She'd spoken without thinking but seeing the despair deepen on Jean-Luc's face—the look of loss and longing in his eyes—she immediately regretted it.

'I didn't know—we couldn't change things!' she said, and knew he understood when he nodded, but although he'd come to talk to Joe, he now said goodbye, his departure not affecting Joe in the slightest, so intent was he on his task.

Lauren followed Jean-Luc down the hall where she stopped him with a touch on the shoulder. He turned and took her in his arms and held her close.

'Now it *would* be pity,' he said, the words muffled by her hair as he'd spoken with his lips against her neck.

'No, it wouldn't be,' she said. 'I feel regret that you missed so much of Joe's life, but not pity for you, Jean-Luc. You are far too strong a man to generate that kind of emotion in a woman.'

He raised his head and looked at her in the dim light of the passage.

'You think so?'

'I'm sure of it. You have mapped out your path and you follow it, in spite of sidetracks and diversions. Jeremy's death was terrible, particularly because right now it's inexplicable, but think of all the children your work has saved.'

He smiled but there was little joy in the expression.

'You can't balance the living against the dead, Lauren,' he said, 'as if one death equals fifteen children saved. But you are right, it isn't self-pity or thoughts of myself that is destroying my sleep, but what happened. I have been over it with Alex and over and over it again in my head and there is nothing to explain what happened. Even last night, when I should have been taking Joe to Cubs, we were meeting, Alex, Phil, Maggie and I, at Scoozi to discuss it with his mother. Jeremy had had cardiac catheterisation before, and the catheter hadn't reached his heart. The septal occluder hadn't been introduced—that little boy's death is a mystery.'

The information about the meeting made Lauren feel about an inch tall! If only she'd seen the other team members!

But right now she had to comfort the man she was coming to love.

'And while it's a mystery you worry about other children—other procedures?'

His arms were linked around her waist so they stood with their bodies touching, but she knew his mind was on work, not on the attraction between them, for all it might have been stirring her senses.

'I would,' he said, frowning now, 'if I hadn't done similar procedures hundreds of times. What bothers me is that we somehow failed Jeremy in our pre-op tests—that he had an underlying condition we didn't know about.'

'But he was a referral from another hospital. You can't be expected to start again from scratch and test him for every condition known to science.'

His arms tightened and he hugged her closer.

'You wouldn't think so but if we discover the cause was an underlying condition, maybe we have to change our ways with outside referrals. Alex and Phil have been discussing that today.'

'Mum! I'm finished.'

Joe's call broke them apart, but Lauren was pleased to find Jean-Luc following her back into the kitchen.

'Your flat is very quiet this evening,' he said, as he settled into a chair beside Joe. 'Usually someone is dropping in, or I can hear your mother moving about upstairs in her flat.'

'Mum's at the gallery, bugging the director about the positioning of her paintings for her next showing, and Russ and Bill are both working.'

'Will you help me put the cards in envelopes?' Joe asked Jean-Luc, pushing the pile of cards and envelopes along the table.

'I will help but I won't do them all,' he said, halving the pile and pushing one half back to Joe. 'But it was a good try,' he added, and Joe smiled his delight.

His stubby fingers struggled with the simple exercise, but with his friend John at his side he kept going until the job was done.

'Bedtime,' Lauren said, and felt rather than saw Jean-Luc's gaze switch from Joe to her.

'You want to read the story?' she asked, and though Jean-Luc agreed, especially as Joe had added his pleas, Lauren knew it wasn't Joe's bedtime that had been in Jean-Luc's mind.

But what to do?

The night they'd made love she'd crept from his bed in the early hours of the morning, hurrying home, uncomfortable about leaving Joe with her mother overnight. But the idea of Jean-Luc staying over at her place was even more disturbing.

Especially right now, when she wanted whatever it was going on between them unnoticed. It was too new, too fragile, and its future definitely too uncertain for her to want to share it, let alone for it to become hospital gossip.

All at once she understood why she hadn't included mention of Jean-Luc in her emails home. She'd been enjoying being in love so much she'd wanted to hold it to herself.

In love?

She stood in the bedroom door as Jean-Luc read a story about a very sleepy wombat to Joe, and tried to work out if what she felt for the man was love. She understood the love she felt for Joe, and her mother, and Russ, and even Bill, but what she felt for Jean-Luc was different.

Joe fell asleep at the same time as the wombat and Jean-Luc put down the book and came quietly out of the room.

He pulled the bedroom door closed behind him, and once again took Lauren in his arms.

'Things might have been so different,' he said, then he kissed her, but with no hint of regret for what might have been. This kiss was for now, and as it deepened and heat burned through her body, causing tremors in her flesh, Lauren forgot the puzzling aspects of love and gave in to the physical delight of kissing Jean-Luc.

'Presumably you have a bedroom,' he eventually murmured, and she eased away from him, aware her clothing was twisted and her hair a wild muddle about her head.

'I have and it even has a bed, but…'

She hesitated, unsure how to put her concerns into words, certain they would sound pathetic.

'You have reservations? About me, perhaps?

'Not about you,' she assured him, still trying to find the words she needed to explain.

Or is it? Is it Jean-Luc in particular or relationships in general? I haven't handled other relationships particularly well, and for all you think you love him, this could well be some leftover attraction from the past—stuff my body remembers but my mind doesn't!

Her mind was off on a tangent, debating, and Jean-Luc was talking again.

'You are worried about your family perhaps. Do they know I am Joe's father?'

'Yes, they know that much.'

'And you do not wish them to know more?'

'What more is there to know?' Lauren demanded, so irritated by this conversation—and by the fact she couldn't freely and easily make love to Jean-Luc—she wanted to hit out, to hurt. 'It's not as if our relationship is going anywhere. You said as much yourself.'

'But it could still be a relationship,' he pointed out. 'We are as attracted to each other as we were when we first met. We are adults, so surely we can enjoy where that attraction leads.'

Put like that it made Lauren's objections seem petty—or maybe childish.

'OK,' she agreed, 'you're right, but—'

She took his hand.

'Let's sit in the kitchen,' she suggested, but looking at him, so at ease in her kitchen—so darned at home—it didn't make things any easier.

'When I came home,' she began, although she knew this wasn't where she should have begun, 'the family closed around me, cared for me. It took me a long time first to gain the confidence I needed to be independent…'

She smiled at him and shrugged. 'OK, so living in a flat beneath my mother and my brother isn't hugely independent, but that was for Joe's sake more than mine. And I *am* independent. But relationships—well, there's Joe, you see. He's not stupid.'

'You do not want men sleeping over in your house and Joe seeing them next morning—that is what you're trying to say?'

She nodded, so embarrassed now her throat had closed up, although she had to get her thoughts said somehow.

'And having you sneak out in the middle of the night—well, that doesn't seem right either.' Her voice was a bit squeaky, but at least she'd got it out, then, realising she'd sounded rude, she added, 'Not right for you, as if I'm ashamed of you when I'm not.'

He stood up and came around the table, taking her in his arms.

'I understand what you are saying,' he said. 'I will not stay tonight, but we will work out something else that suits us both. And now, if I am not mistaken, that is your mother's car coming down the back lane, and knowing her she will tap on your door before she goes up to her flat so I had better go.'

He smoothed his hands across her hair, then kissed her hard on her lips, his hands now mussing up her hair again.

'When is the exhibition?'

'A week on Friday—drinks and nibbles at six. Would you like to come? We go along en masse, Mum and I, Russ and Bill, various neighbours who are hospital folk.'

'I would love to attend but that is the day the toxicology report is due—I may be tied up with Alex and Phil.'

The words were so full of pain Lauren wanted to kiss him again but, as he had surmised, her mother was already knocking on the front door of the flat.

She gave him a quick goodnight kiss, touching his face for he was looking worried again, no doubt thinking of the meeting that lay ahead.

The mood in the team meeting the next morning was grim, particularly as it was attended by various members of the hospital hierarchy and a member of the hospital's legal firm.

'This is not an inquisition,' Alex began, 'is simply an opportunity to put every stage of the event into writing.'

Lauren glanced at Jean-Luc and saw him pale at the

word 'event'. But she could hardly offer sympathy in this situation—not that he'd have accepted it anyway.

'Lauren,' Alex continued, 'let's begin with you. Jeremy came in when, and who was with him?'

'He was admitted at six the evening before the operation so we could ensure he went nil by mouth from midnight. According to his mother, he'd had a meal at four-thirty. On arrival at the hospital, he was put into bed and watched television until eight-thirty. Mrs Willis came in with him and was provided with a reclining chair so she could stay the night, which was what she wished to do.'

Lauren closed her eyes as she tried to picture the events of that evening.

'Jeremy was restless and thirsty and had a small drink of water at nine. He had no medication at all that night. I was going off duty as Mrs Willis had asked me to be present at the operation. I checked Jeremy before I left the hospital at ten and he and Mrs Willis were both sleeping soundly.'

'Why do you say soundly?' Jean-Luc asked, and Lauren turned to face him, wondering why she *had* said the word, again recalling images of the evening.

'He was breathing deeply, not snoring but making those snuffly noises as he breathed in, giving the impression he was deeply asleep.'

Everyone, even the legal eagle, nodded their understanding, and Alex called on Jasmine, who'd been on duty overnight, to give her account of the night.

'He slept all night. I wasn't beside his bed the whole time, but I checked him regularly, as did the other nurses on duty. You can see from his chart that someone went in every hour and recorded the fact that he was asleep.'

And so it went, all the accounts recorded to be transcribed later and signed by the various staff involved. And as they grew closer to the moment when Jeremy's heart had stopped beating, the tension in the room grew and grew until Lauren at least began to find it unbearable.

'We'll break for coffee,' Alex decreed, and Lauren shot him a relieved smile, certain he, too, had been feeling more and more uncomfortable. She hoped the break would give her a chance to speak to Jean-Luc but he had buttonholed Alex as soon as the break was announced and the two took their coffee to a corner of the room, obviously wanting a private conversation.

Fifteen minutes later the meeting continued, everyone giving statements so the entire operation was documented from at least six and sometimes a dozen points of view.

'The frustrating thing,' Lauren said to Jean-Luc when they found themselves going down in the lift together, 'is that we might now have it all recorded but we're no closer to finding answers.'

'We might be,' Jean-Luc said, and he sounded so positive Lauren stared at him.

'You've an idea?' she asked, and he shook his head.

'The shadow of one, nothing more, but having a record of everything that happened means we can refer to it when we have more information to hand. Dinner?'

The question, coming as it did, made little sense.

'Dinner?' Lauren repeated, not sure she'd heard right.

Jean-Luc smiled and she felt her knees buckle.

'I thought maybe you didn't have a previous engagement, and it's not Cub night, and that being the case you might join me for dinner, not at Scoozi, as half the hospital is always there, but perhaps at one of the restaurants we drive past when we go to Coogee.'

Dinner at Coogee with Jean-Luc?

Lauren could feel excitement building in her chest, and a different excitement building lower down.

Would he ask her to stay the night?

Time to pack a toothbrush?

'Well?'

Now heat rose in her cheeks and she was glad they'd finally reached the ground floor and she could hurry out of the lift so he wouldn't see her blushing at her thoughts.

She turned back to him and smiled.

'Sounds good,' she said. 'I'll have to check someone's available to mind Joe, but that shouldn't be a problem. What time?'

He didn't return her smile and she began to wonder if she'd misread the invitation, but when he took her by the elbow and ushered her towards a relatively quiet corner of the corridor there was no mistaking the gleam of desire in his eyes, or his intent in the huskiness of his words.

'Early, say seven, so we can walk on the beach before we go home to bed.'

'Home to bed?' she whispered, her own voice as husky as his.

Now he smiled.

'Home to bed,' he repeated, then he touched a finger to her lips. 'It's time we got to know each other better. You said Joe often stays over with your mother or Russ. He will be all right? Will it worry you to arrange that? Embarrass you?'

Would it?

Her mother would definitely understand—hadn't she been urging Lauren to get to know Jean-Luc better?

Although making love to him might not have been in her mind when she'd said it…

Lauren watched the man in question stride away, obviously not heading home as she was. But she was reasonably certain she could pack a toothbrush in her handbag, and a certain sense of daring flooded through her.

'Over thirty and getting excited about spending the night with a man!' she muttered to herself as she left the hospital. Then she excused herself, smiling as she added, 'Well, it *is* the first time.'

'First time for what?'

Bill asked the question as he linked his arm through hers, walking with her to the lights while she wondered just how loudly she'd been speaking.

She turned to Bill. He was family as well as being a dear friend.

'First time I've spent the night with a man,' she admitted, blushing and laughing at the same time. 'And it hasn't happened yet, and knowing the way fate plays around with me and Jean-Luc it might not, but I don't want to be sneaking around you and Russ and Mum so it's best you all know, but it's private, Bill, I don't want it all over the hospital.'

The lights changed and they crossed the road.

'You know Russ and I would never spread gossip—we've suffered enough to loathe the very word, but are you sure, Lorie? Sure it's what you want?'

Bill was the only person who'd ever called her Lorie, and she knew it was out of the deep love he felt for her. Knew also that his question came out of that love…

She stopped on the footpath and turned so he could see her face as she answered.

'I'm sure for me, Bill,' she said, and read understanding in his soft brown eyes. 'As far as Jean-Luc's concerned, well, I don't think he knows himself. He's had so many shocks—finding me alive and discovering he's a father. Those two things were enough to throw his world into chaos. With Jeremy's death on top of it—well, I doubt he's able to think rationally at all. But if all he has to offer to me is an affair, then I'm willing to take it, because at least this time I'll have some memories of our time together.'

Bill put his arm around her shoulder and gave her a hug, and as they moved down the street towards home, he sighed.

'Well, there are two good shoulders here ready for you if you need a cry later,' he said. 'But you're right. If you don't take the chance now, you'll have to live with regrets, and memories are far better company than regrets.'

Bill's words confirmed her own thoughts and it was with mounting excitement she dressed for her 'date'. A real dress—Jean-Luc hadn't seen her in a dress. Not that she had many, but this one, a soft cotton with a V-neck and a swirly skirt, pale green with smudgy patterns of darker green and blue all over it, was her favourite.

She brushed her hair until it shone and thought about pinning it on top of her head—she could do sophistication when required—but then remembered how Jean-Luc loved to touch her hair and left it down, hanging in two long curtains from her centre parting.

At seven he was at the door. Joe was already settled in her mother's flat—Jean-Luc was *her* date.

And he was gorgeous! Not that his clothes were anything out of the ordinary—black jeans that fitted his body like a second skin, and a dark blue polo shirt in some kind of silky fabric that clung lovingly to his muscled shoulders and was open enough for a few dark hairs to show on his chest.

Lauren wanted to touch but didn't, revelling instead in the glow of appreciation in his eyes.

'You are a very beautiful woman,' he said quietly, then he took her hand. 'Shall we go?'

It was only as he led her down the garden path—down the garden path? her mind echoed—that she recovered enough of her senses to remember her car was parked in the lane out the back.

'We're going the wrong way,' she said, and he smiled and pointed to a dark limousine waiting outside the gate.

'I thought tonight we'd go in style,' he said. 'The driver has also suggested a restaurant and made a booking for us.'

Lauren stared at the man who had made all these arrangements in such a short time. There had to be a catch.

'And our walk on the beach?'

Jean-Luc smiled again.

'He will wait. He is ours to command—at least until midnight—but I have a feeling we won't need to keep him out that late.'

The look in his eyes was enough to take Lauren's excitement from hectic to feverish, so much so she actually shivered.

Had Jean-Luc seen it that he put his arm around her as he led her to the limo? The driver was now out of the car and holding the back door open for his passengers.

Bill had put his arm around her shoulders earlier—a comforting arm. This arm was possessive, and the thought of that possession—what lay ahead—churned in Lauren's stomach.

'Champagne?'

Jean-Luc had opened a small cabinet in the back of the vehicle and produced a bottle of what looked like very expensive champagne.

'French of course,' he teased, but Lauren was unable to speak, spellbound by the magic of it all.

'I feel like Cinderella, whisked away to the ball,' she told him, but she took the flute of champagne he handed her, and touched her glass to his.

'To tonight and all the nights ahead of us,' Jean-Luc proposed, and Lauren understood the toast. This was not a fairy story with a for-ever-and-ever ending, but a short story.

'To memories,' she said, and when he quirked a dark eyebrow at her words, she smiled.

'This time I intend to remember,' she said, and he chuckled.

They dined at a table on a high deck, looking out over the beach and ocean, feeding each other tastes of their desserts, sipping cognac after dinner because it was French and it was that kind of evening.

Then, with shoes shed, they walked on the beach, feeling the sand between their toes and the water sloshing around their feet, not saying much but aware all the time they were putting off the moment of return—putting off the finale of the evening.

But as they settled into the limousine for the ride home, a new shivery sensation ran down Lauren's spine. Where would this lead? The excitement she'd felt earlier built again and she rubbed her hand against Jean-Luc's chest.

Memories! She'd have memories!

Slowly, slowly—he wanted to love her slowly and completely. Jean-Luc had promised himself that. But she was so open and trusting and so gloriously giving that his excitement was hard to keep under control.

Lauren naked in his bed, her hands exploring his body.

He knew from the tentative movements that she was inexperienced in love and he wanted the experience to be memorable for her, but control was impossible when she was so deliciously excited, so deliriously exciting.

But still he tried, exploring her body with his lips, feeling her shudder of reaction as he kissed her neck, her shiver of anticipation when he fondled her breast.

'You are a source of such delight,' he whispered, his tongue twisting in her belly button. 'Soft skin, full breasts, firm butt—I want to love every inch of you, sweet Lauren.'

'And when it's my turn?' she asked, her voice muffled because her lips were pressed against his hair, her own falling around his face like a curtain of privacy.

'Do you want a turn?' he asked, more excitement building.

'To kiss your body? Of course!'

And she moved so she was leaning over him, her breasts falling to his chest.

'Where shall I start? Here?'

She kissed his neck, in the hollow where it joined his shoulder.

'Or here?'

She teased her tongue across one of his nipples.

'Or here?'

Her tongue probed his navel, sending shooting signals southward.

Then she moved again and this time her voice was husky with excitement.

'Or here?'

And tentatively she took his penis in her hand, and slid her lips across it then she opened her mouth and took the tip inside, sliding her tongue around it, nibbling gently with her teeth as he had nibbled on her nipple.

Jean-Luc stood the pleasure of it for as long as he could then eased away, pushing her back on the bed.

'Torture, sheer torture, my temptress,' he said. 'Enough teasing, we will make love. I was going slowly so it would be good for you, but if you get me any more excited then slowly will be impossible.'

'I don't need slowly, or expect that it will be good for me every time, Jean-Luc,' his temptress told him, her hand resting against his cheek. 'I may not be experienced, or remember what experience I did have, but I've read plenty of books. Making love with you will give me pleasure whether my toes tingle or not.'

Jean-Luc looked down into her shadowed face and shook his head. He had a feeling in his heart he didn't understand, and right now, with his body rampant with desire, was not the time to be analysing it.

'Your toes will tingle,' he growled, then he kissed her, demanding a response and revelling in it when it came. They were making love on equal terms, the teasing done, the excitement of the act building and building until he heard her gasp and felt her shudder of release and he let himself fall into the abyss that opened up in front of him, landing safely in his lovely Lauren's arms.

His lovely Lauren?

The thought returned to him when he woke in the night and looked at the naked woman curled in sleep beside him, her hair a dark splash on the pillow, enough light from outside for him to see the hint of a smile on her lips.

Satisfaction?

He hoped so.

But *his* lovely Lauren?

This was an affair. He'd told her so. True, there was the

problem of Joe but he had already worked that out in his mind. Joe could spend his holidays in France. He could afford to fly both Joe and Lauren over a couple of times a year. And in between he could make trips to Australia. His parents, too, could visit. He'd buy a unit here in Sydney so the family had a base. His mother would be proud to see Joe as a Nipper.

And Lauren?

He drifted back to sleep, content now to know she'd be there in the morning. They could make love again.

CHAPTER NINE

IT WAS if they were a real family, Lauren thought, watching Jean-Luc help Joe with his 'homework' later that week. The task was to match pictures to words and although Lauren knew Joe could do it without help, he was obviously enjoying the attention of his friend John so was deliberately getting things wrong and turning it into a game.

Even Lucy seemed to be accepting Jean-Luc, still standing by Joe's side while Jean-Luc was in the house but no longer making dark, growly, keep-away noises in his throat.

As for her own life…

She gave a little sigh of satisfaction. Because Joe was used to sleeping in his little bedroom in her mother's flat when Lauren did night duty, it was easy to settle him there for the night. Then she and Jean-Luc would wander back to his place, sometimes walking through the park first, sometimes going out for a meal, but usually cutting short the time between leaving Joe and getting into bed, for their love-making was so exciting that just thinking about it sent feathery tremors along Lauren's nerves.

Homework finished, Jean-Luc stood up.

'Read me a story?' Joe asked, knowing it was his bedtime.

'Not tonight, little friend,' Jean-Luc said, ruffling his son's hair. 'Tonight I have a meeting at the hospital.'

Lauren felt a slight dampening of her excitement. Had he told her that? She tried to think, but thinking of anything apart from getting back into bed with Jean-Luc was becoming difficult.

He'd certainly mentioned a meeting, but tonight?

He left Joe at the kitchen table and walked through to the common foyer. Lauren had the front door open and was leaning on the jamb.

'I will see you later?' he asked quietly.

Of course he would. She was besotted. Wild horses wouldn't keep her away.

But she tried for cool, calm and collected as she asked, 'How much later?'

He gave the cheeky grin she loved so much.

'Not much later,' he promised. 'Ten o'clock. I'll call down here for you.'

'There's no need. I could wait at your place.'

He'd given her a key but she'd never used it. This seemed like the ideal time. But he was frowning and shaking his head.

'No, I will call for you,' he said. 'I would not like you being in the flat on your own.'

A feeling of warmth stole through her. Surely if he was concerned for her safety— No, she didn't want to start thinking that way.

'I'll be waiting,' she promised and, after a quick glance to see there was no one in the street outside, she put her arms around him and gave him a kiss.

Which had just begun to get interesting when Joe came racing down the passageway.

'John, John, you didn't get the invitation.'

He handed the blue envelope with stickers stuck all over it to Jean-Luc and as he took it, thanking Joe, bending over to assure him he wouldn't miss the party for the world, memories Lauren had thought lost for ever rushed over her, swamping her with details—a child with an envelope for Jean-Luc, hearts all over it. *Je t'aime.*

A return address!

Therese Fournier!

'The envelope—you got a letter from your wife. We fought!' she said, staring at the man who'd been the man she'd loved. 'You didn't tell me *that* when you told me how you'd fallen in love with me in India! You told me all about our time together and didn't think it sufficiently important to tell me you'd been married at the time? That must be why I blocked that bit of memory—blocked *you* out. The specialists said it was some other trauma! You were married all along and you were cheating on her with me—'

'Lauren—' Jean-Luc began, but too many memories were now crowding in Lauren's head, pounding at her brain—hurting…

'You've got a meeting, you'd better go,' she said.

Had Lucy heard the despair in Lauren's voice that she now began to bark?

'Lauren—' Jean-Luc said again, but Lauren held up her hand.

'Just go, Jean-Luc, I need to think.'

'I can't leave you like this—you're in shock.'

But attracted by Lucy's noise, Russ came down the stairs, while her mother's door was opening on the first floor.

'There are plenty of people here who can deal with shock,' Lauren told him. 'You've got a meeting, remember.'

He looked confused, but no more confused than Lauren felt as so many memories came pushing out of whatever dark corner had held them trapped.

'Ten o'clock?' he asked quietly as she opened the door for him and he walked out.

'I don't think so,' she managed, the mess in her head making her feel physically sick.

He walked away and Lauren turned to face her family.

'I've remembered things,' she said. 'And now I'm going to bed. Will someone, please, read Joe his story?'

No one said a word and the silence seemed to echo along the hall and up the stairs, then Joe said, 'Gran will,' and hurried up the stairs to where Gran was standing by her door.

Was there a strange note in his voice?

Surely not fear!

Yet it had been his act of handing Jean-Luc the envelope that had opened the floodgates and Lauren's reaction could have shocked her child.

Seeing his uncertainty shook Lauren out of her welter of self-absorption and she hurried after her child.

'Oh, I'm sorry, Joe, darling. I didn't mean I didn't want to read your story. But I have a headache and I need to lie down.'

It wasn't quite a lie. She could feel a headache looming—and it was going to be a doozy.

She gave Joe a goodnight kiss, ignored the adults all watching her with questioning yet cautious looks and walked back into her flat towards her bedroom. Perhaps when she was lying down, the past would go back to where it belonged and she could sort out how to go forward into the future.

'Don't lock your door,' she heard Russ order. 'I want to check on you later.'

She didn't answer, but didn't lock her door. Her family were too good to her for her to shut them out. But lying down only made the headache worse and in the end she had to resort to one of the strong painkillers she'd been using far less frequently of late. Indeed, sometimes lately it had seemed she might be completely cured of the vicious pain that pressed against her temples and hammered in her head—cured of the pain if not the memory loss.

By morning the headache was gone and although she felt as if she'd been run over by a bus, a not unusual after-effect of the painkiller, she headed off to work, knowing she'd be better off thinking about her patients than trying to work out whether the past had any relevance to her present life.

She was reasonably sure it did, but while she could function on a day-to-day level, she knew she wasn't up to sorting out the emotional mess she was in, so work was definitely the answer.

She walked up the road, deliberately not looking at number twenty-six, for how could she see the house and not think of Jean-Luc? Back in India he had betrayed her—not only her but his wife as well—and now he'd betrayed her again, by not telling her of the fight they'd had—by pretending they'd still been in a loving relationship when they'd parted.

What *could* she believe?

Was he still married?

Was that why he'd been at pains to tell her their relationship wouldn't lead to marriage?

Probably!

Depression joined the confusion in her head, so she strode out, determined to forget it all, to put the entire experience behind her—letting anger feed in to burn her other thoughts away. If *that man* thought he was going to lay claim to Joe, he had another think coming!

Becky was down in the unit, delivering some file notes.

'Did you hear?' she asked Lauren.

Lauren stared at her and snapped, 'Hear what?' Not caring much what was happening anywhere.

'About Jeremy? I don't know for sure what they've found out but there's a meeting going on upstairs with Alex and Jean-Luc and the hospital bigwigs and the solicitor. They know what happened!'

Concern for the man she kept telling herself she didn't love tightened Lauren's chest. Would a hospital solicitor protect Jean-Luc or throw him to the wolves?

'I hope they're not going to pin the blame on Jean-Luc,' she heard herself say. Weak! Pathetically weak! Yet still she persisted. 'I know the hospital hierarchy—they'll be looking for a scapegoat and because he's temporary staff he'd fit right in with the plans.'

'Oh, so we fancy the dishy French doctor, do we?' Becky teased, and Lauren realised, belatedly, her defence of Jean-Luc must have come out far too strongly.

But she could still protest, 'It's not that, but I was there—he did nothing wrong. The catheter hadn't even reached the heart. It's just that hospital management can be so devious, blaming him is just the kind of thing they'd do.'

'You're right, but I doubt he's in strife,' Becky said. 'It was something to do with the toxicology report that made them all excited.'

And as Jean-Luc hadn't administered any drugs, that let him out, Lauren realised, feeling far more relieved than she should have.

She said goodbye to Becky and got on with her work, which today was in the post-op room where the babies and children were nursed and monitored while they came out of the anaesthetic after their operations.

She looked at the operating list. Phil was operating first, a three-month-old with an atrioventricular canal defect. Phil would be closing the holes between the atria and ventricles and dividing the common valve presently in the heart into two valves so each of the ventricles had a valve into their respective atria. It was delicate work but had such a high success rate everyone was always optimistic about the op.

Although after Jeremy the mood of optimism was sadly lacking in the unit—one death affecting so many people.

Later in the day, Alex—and undoubtedly Jean-Luc—would be doing another TGA. As often happened in the unit when you got one case of a particular defect, you got a run of them.

Lauren went through to the post-op room, and began to prepare for the arrival of her small patients, checking first the monitors were working, then making sure all the drugs they could possibly need were close to hand.

Then all she had to do was wait, which was a problem because not being busy meant she had time to think.

Maybe if she thought about Jeremy and what the toxicology report might have said.

But she didn't know enough about drugs and their reactions to even begin to guess what might be happening, so she was left with sorting through her memories.

Yes, she did remember walking on the beach with Jean-Luc, and being with the children from the orphanage. She could see Father Joe's kindly face, unlined except for smile lines radiating out from his eyes, his skin unmarked despite the fact he was close to eighty.

And now she could remember how he looked, and even recall his soft Irish voice, she felt the pain of loss and knew she had to grieve for him. And for the children—faces and names coming back to her, the smiles of the babies as she picked them up to cuddle them, the toddlers clamouring for a story.

So many lost, such innocents who surely hadn't deserved to die.

She blinked back tears and sniffed hard, but the tears kept coming and as she found a tissue and scrubbed at her cheeks and pressed it against her eyes she wondered if she was crying for Father Joe and the children or because she'd also remembered what had happened between her and Jean-Luc?

Most tears are tears of self-pity, she heard Father Joe say. He'd told her that when she'd cried for a baby who'd died. *Remember that,* he'd said. *It is good to grieve, to cry even, but be sure you're crying for the baby, not because it makes you sad she died.*

And as Lauren sat and waited for another baby to be given into her care, she considered his words and finally decided there'd be no more tears—not for the past, or the present. Jean-Luc had proved in the past not to be the man she'd thought he was, so why would he have changed?

The arrival of little Tracey Oliver got her mind focussed on work. Tracey was on an ECMO machine. The extracorporeal membrane oxygenation machine wasn't always used after open-heart surgery but Tracey's operation must have been serious enough for the surgical team to decide her battered little heart needed the extra help. During the operation, when Tracey had been connected to the heart-lung machine, she'd had tubes placed directly into the large blood vessels near her heart, one to carry venous blood into the bypass machine where it had been oxygenated and returned to her body through a tube into her aorta.

'Knowing she wasn't doing well, Phil left the tubes in place and put her straight onto the ECMO when he was finished,' Maggie, the anaesthetist who'd accompanied Tracey to post-op, explained. 'Just keep watch for any signs of bleeding and on her blood oxygenation. Phil hates having his patients on ECMO but Tracey was so weak before the op he had no choice.'

Lauren assured Maggie she'd be extra-watchful, and she looked at the little girl and wondered if they'd be able to get her off the machine before too long. Complications multiplied the longer patients needed the special help. Haemorrhages in the brain because the blood had to be kept thinned so it went through the machine, infections and kidney failure were all common if a patient needed ECMO for more than a couple of days.

Maggie left, promising to return in half an hour, then Theo came in, wanting to check the adjustment on the machine.

'As soon as her heart is pumping more strongly we can cut down on the blood flow through the machine,' he said, reading a printout from the monitor.

'Well, at least she's in good hands with you here,' Lauren told him. Kurt, who'd been in charge of the heart-lung machine and the ECMO machines when the unit had first opened, had been an excellent operator, but Theo had a different approach. For him the patient was more important than the machine and he was forever tinkering with the machines in order to get better outcomes for his patients.

'Good hands with all of us, Lauren,' Theo responded. 'We're a team, remember.'

'You're very chatty this morning,' Lauren told him, not wanting to think about the team—or one particular member of it. 'Could it be some of the love dust that falls in this place from time to time has settled on you and the new South African surgeon?'

He looked at Lauren and frowned.

'What makes you ask that?' he demanded.

She was taken aback by his response—the stiff, unbending, manly Greek suddenly very much in evidence.

'I just thought you liked her,' Lauren said, aware how lame it sounded.

'I can like her without there being anything in it,' Theo retorted. 'Certainly without there being any of this love-dust nonsense you're carrying on about anyway.'

'Well, forgive me for living,' Lauren snapped. 'I thought we were friends and could talk about things.'

He gave her a look that would have burnt toast and stalked out of the room.

Lauren concentrated on Tracey. The day had not got off to a good start and now seemed intent on getting worse.

'You're still Joe's father and you can keep on seeing him as you've been doing,' she said to Jean-Luc when he met her as she left the PICU at the end of the day.

'And you? What am I to you?' he demanded, and Lauren looked at him and shook her head.

'I haven't worked that out yet,' she admitted, 'but if we look at it the other way—at what I am to you—it's easier because I was never going to be more to you than the other half of an affair while you were in Sydney. You told me that the first night we made love. And now, thinking about what happened in the past, well, I'm not sure you're the man I thought you were—and that means I'm not sure I want to have an affair with you.'

They were standing in the PICU tearoom which, miraculously, was empty, although Jean-Luc was only too aware they could be interrupted at any minute.

Not that he was thinking about interruptions! Lauren's intransigent stance had left him stunned—in fact, stunned just about summed up his mental state over the past twenty-four hours, what with one thing and another.

'I need to talk to you, about the past. I need to explain some things. Can we at least discuss this somewhere more sensible?' he asked, sure they could find a way through the tangle they'd somehow managed to tie around themselves.

'More sensible like the beach?' Lauren snapped. 'Or your bedroom perhaps? I don't think so. I don't want to listen to any more of your lies, Jean-Luc.'

And with that she walked away.

But it was Cubs night and although he'd had precious little sleep the previous night, at least that would give him an excuse to see Lauren again—although that would never be his prime reason for wanting to take Joe to Cubs.

He loved seeing the little boy in his uniform and seeing the pride in his eyes when he joined his six and made his responses at the beginning of the meeting.

Things may have all gone wrong between him and Lauren—and he hadn't understood her anger the first time so how could he understand it now?—but Joe was a gift he'd unexpectedly received and whatever happened he had to continue to build his relationship with his son.

'Where's your mother?' he asked, when Joe, all ready to depart, answered the front door that evening.

'She's got a headache, but Russ is here. He's been minding me until you came,' Joe told him, then, unconcerned by any vibes of tension Jean-Luc might have been sending out, he turned to tell Lucy to stay and mind the house.

'I'd better see Russ, then, and tell him we're going,' Jean-Luc said, wondering if Lauren really did have a headache or if she was using the classic excuse.

'Is Lauren OK?' he asked, as he followed Joe into the kitchen of the flat and found Russ busy on his laptop at the kitchen table. 'Theo said she gets headaches still—from her injury in the typhoon?'

Russ didn't reply immediately, finishing what he was doing and hitting the save button, but when he did look up there was no hint of animosity in his face.

More like concern.

'She hasn't had them badly for a while, but remembering those lost six weeks, well, it seems to have brought them back.'

Jean-Luc nodded understandingly, but apparently that didn't satisfy his lover's older brother.

'They'd be good memories, wouldn't they?' he asked.

'John, we'll be late,' Joe urged, but Jean-Luc knew he had to answer. Not only answer, but tell the truth.

'For me they were the best, and I think for Lauren also, although—at the end—we argued, Russ, and I think that might be bothering her.'

Russ considered this for a moment, then shrugged.

'She'll sort it out. She's an exceedingly strong young woman, our Lauren,' he said. 'Now, you'd better get the brat to Cubs.'

'Not a brat,' Joe answered automatically, but he gave Russ a high-five and Lucy a last hug and kiss before taking Jean-Luc's hand and leading him out the back to where Lauren's little car was parked.

'Mum gave me the keys to mind,' he said, his chubby hand opening to reveal the car keys.

Without the heart!

This was not good!

Russ had said Lauren would work things out—but would that be in Jean-Luc's favour?

And what did he want anyway?

Hadn't she been right to remind him he'd only wanted an affair?

Didn't he?

'Come on, John,' Joe urged, and Jean-Luc put aside all thoughts of Lauren and concentrated on getting one small Cub safely to his meeting.

Lauren heard the car drive off, and though she dozed—the headache was genuine and the tablets made her sleepy—she also heard it return. She could hear Joe's excited voice relating all that had happened at the meeting, and Russ's voice as well—so he'd waited until Joe came home. But she couldn't tell if Jean-Luc was still in her kitchen—he often stayed to put Joe to bed and read his story.

The tablet and the sleep had eased her headache enough that she should be able to think. But trying to sort out the muddle in her head was impossible. She needed to get out of the house, have a long walk on the beach—no, not on the beach, perhaps in the park.

'Stupid idea,' she muttered to herself. 'You could walk from here to Melbourne and still not sort things out.'

She picked up her mobile and phoned Bill.

'Are you in my flat with Russ?' she asked.

'I am,' Bill replied cautiously.

'Is Jean-Luc there?'

'He is.'

'Damn. Never mind. You know the shoulder you offered—could I borrow it? I need to sort things out in my head. Can we walk in the park? Can you get away? I can slip out the front door and wait across the road.'

'Yes, yes and yes.' Bill must have kept her questions in sequence in his head. 'I'll be there in a few minutes.'

She pictured him making some excuse to the family and their visitor. In fact, all he needed to say was 'hospital' and no one would question him.

They walked in silence at first, Bill obviously waiting for some input from her before he spoke.

Some input! What she finally managed was, 'I'm *so* muddled, Bill! I can't believe it.'

'Because of memories?' he asked gently.

And she sighed and admitted he was right.

'Bad memories of Jean-Luc?' he prompted.

'Bad memories of how we parted.' And she went on to explain about Joe handing Jean-Luc the envelope and the picture flashing so vividly—so clearly—in her head—a child handing Jean-Luc an envelope.

'It was a love letter from his wife back in France— Jean-Luc was married all along,' Lauren explained.

'Did you *know* that or just guess?'

'He didn't deny it.'

Bill sighed.

'It isn't my shoulder you need,' he said, 'but Jean-Luc's ear. You need to talk this through with him, Lorie, you know that.'

It was her turn to sigh.

'But to him my reaction doesn't make sense.'

'Then maybe he's not the man for you.'

'He isn't anyway,' Lauren snapped, angry because she knew Bill was right. 'He doesn't want commitment—oh, he'll commit to Joe and sort out some kind of access to him but me, I'm just a diversion.'

They walked some more.

'Maybe you should find out why,' Bill said, then he pointed ahead and Lauren realised they'd walked in a circle and were back across the road from their houses. 'His light's on. Go and talk to him.'

She was about to protest that it was his bedroom light and she didn't want to talk to him there when she realised she couldn't reveal such weakness, even to Bill. But reluctantly she walked across the road and rang the doorbell. He'd have to come into the foyer to answer the door—they could talk in the sitting room.

'Lauren?'

His voice was cool and suddenly Bill's suggestion seemed ridiculous. Jean-Luc didn't have a problem—she did, and it was something she had to sort out by herself.

'Thank you for taking Joe to Cubs,' she said, her knees shaking with tension that was building and building.

'It was my pleasure. Do you want to come in?'

Of course she wanted to come in! She wanted to be drawn into his arms and into his bed and wanted to be so lost in love-making she need never think again.

'I don't think so,' she muttered, still standing like a stork on his front doormat.

'We could talk.'

Did his voice sound strained?

No, she was imagining it because she wanted this to be as hard for him as it was for her.

'About India? About the letter? About Therese?'

He sighed.

'I'm sorry, Lauren, but it was all a very long time ago, and as you wouldn't listen to my explanation back then and as I didn't get much sleep last night, I doubt very much we will be able to sort things out tonight, but if you want to talk about it, fine.'

He looked strained as well, the scars on his cheeks standing out as they did when he was tired, but she couldn't let pity undermine her anger.

'There was no explanation that would be acceptable,' she said. 'You didn't understand that then and you don't seem to now. We're not only from different cultures but we have totally different values. Fidelity and trust are important things to me and obviously they aren't to you. Goodnight!'

And with that she left his doorstep and marched home, aware he was still standing in the doorway, but whether he was watching her or staring into space or even waiting for another freak wave to sweep them both away she didn't know because she refused to give him the satisfaction of turning around for one last look…

* * *

Jean-Luc watched her go, aware he should have called her back and sorted things out between them, but he was too tired—too emotionally drained. He'd allowed himself to become consumed with work, finding that easier to deal with than the situation with Lauren. He'd suspected all along that Rosemary Willis had something apart from Jeremy's death bothering her, but to find out what it was—she had given Jeremy a sleeping pill the night before the operation—and then to deal with it, well, he'd been up most of the night, first talking to Alex and Phil and then, with Maggie's help, trying to comfort the distraught mother. The fact that she'd suspected her actions might have inadvertently led to her son's death was bad enough, but the confirmation, with the toxicology report, was close to destroying her.

So he and Maggie had comforted and counselled her while his own world fell to pieces all around him!

He shook his head. Surely he couldn't be placing such importance on Lauren's anger.

On Lauren herself?

Not when his work had always been his focus—*and* his solace.

A dull ache inside his chest suggested that focus might be shifting but, thoroughly exhausted, he knew he couldn't think about it now.

He went to bed.

CHAPTER TEN

THAT Lauren had become important in his life—and probably always had been—became more apparent as the days passed with no more than a polite nod from her when he was in the PICU or a purely medical discussion if they happened to be together in team meetings.

And while his body ached for her, he suspected the attraction went far beyond the physical, but he had no idea how to bridge the gap between them. Tentative suggestions about dinner when they'd sat on the beach and watched Joe come last in the flag races had met with a cool look and a polite 'I think not' and a request that they sit down and talk had been similarly disregarded.

A week had passed in this way and now he had Joe's birthday party to look forward to—or dread—the following day. He should be on top of the world, work going well, Jeremy Willis's death behind him, about to attend his son's birthday party for the first time, and he was sitting alone in his empty flat, feeling sorry for himself.

'Well, not so much sorry for myself as confused,' he said to the microwave that was heating his frozen meal. 'Now I'm talking to myself like she does—I've got it bad!'

He might have continued the conversation—after all,

microwaves didn't answer back—had not furious barking attracted his attention. It was outside his front door and from the sound of the bark it was Lucy.

Had the dog heard about his break-up with Lauren and come to kill him?

The barking continued and he left the microwave beeping its own message and hurried to the door where, from the sound of things, Lucy was now hurling his body against the panels.

He opened the door and Lucy sprang back, barking and hurrying up the path, so obviously wanting Jean-Luc to follow that he grabbed his door-key from the hook on the wall, shut the door and hurried after the dog.

At number thirty a white-faced Joe stood peering anxiously out the open front door, and at the sight of Jean-Luc he ran forward and threw himself into his arms.

Jean-Luc grabbed his son and held him hard, feeling the little body shaking all over, but Lucy was barking again and, carrying Joe, Jean-Luc walked inside.

An older woman he didn't know was lying on the floor. He knelt beside her and felt a thready pulse, listened for breath sounds, then tipped her on her back to begin expired air resuscitation.

Joe stood and watched, explaining in a tearful voice, Jean-Luc taking in the gist of it while he breathed air into the woman's lungs.

'It's Mrs West, she minds me when everyone is out. She went "Aaargh" and fell down,' Joe explained, watching the procedure with wondering eyes. 'I rang all the Os and told someone number thirty Kensington Terrace but the person kept on asking things I didn't know.'

Joe was crying now and though Jean-Luc longed to

hold and comfort his son, he knew Mrs West was his priority. Besides, Lucy was sitting close to Joe now and he had his arms firmly around the dog's neck so he was getting some comfort.

'You did a great job. You gave the address and they'll send an ambulance,' Jean-Luc told him, praying he was right. They were so close to the hospital he'd soon know and if necessary he could phone again.

He continued breathing while Joe went on to explain he'd sent Lucy to get John and wasn't Lucy clever?

'Very clever!'

Unfortunately it was a police car, not an ambulance, that turned up at number thirty, directed to check if the call had been a hoax. The police constable called for an ambulance, which arrived only minutes later, and Mrs West was attached to oxygen and monitors and wheeled out.

'Now who'll look after me?' Joe asked, as the ambulance drove off.

'I will,' Jean-Luc told him. 'Shall we read a story?'

Even Lucy seemed to approve and while Jean-Luc sat in a big armchair with Joe on his knee, Lucy lay on the floor at their feet, his head resting on Jean-Luc's shoe.

'Although that was probably only so she could bite off my leg if I tried to take Joe away,' Jean-Luc said to Russ who, having been on duty, was the first of the family to arrive back and, seeing the flat door open, had come in.

Jean-Luc had just finished explaining to Russ what had happened when Bill and Lauren arrived, Mrs Henderson having stayed on at the gallery to discuss sales—good sales, according to Bill—with the owner.

'So Mrs West's in hospital. At Big Jimmie's?' Lauren asked.

Jean-Luc nodded, but he smiled at the name given to the adult hospital up the road. All the staff at the children's hospital called the original service Big Jimmie's.

I wish he wouldn't smile, Lauren thought—a totally unnecessary and intrusive thought considering she should be concentrating on Mrs West, her well-being and who in her family to contact.

'I'd better go up to the hospital and see Mrs West,' she said, 'so when I phone the family I can tell them what's happening.'

'I've phoned the hospital—it was a heart attack and she's resting easily now. You stay here and put Joe to bed, he's had a shock,' Russ told her. 'I'll go up to the hospital and deal with whatever we need to deal with there.'

Lauren knew it made sense, but that meant she would have to stay here with Jean-Luc—although Bill was here, or he would have been if he hadn't immediately decided he'd go up to the hospital with Russ.

Resigning herself to her fate, Lauren crossed the room, intending to lift her sleeping son off Jean-Luc's knee, but he forestalled her, standing up with Joe in his arms.

'I'll carry him to his bedroom,' he said. 'You'd better come along. You know better than I do about his pyjamas and things.'

The tiredness in Jean-Luc's voice hurt Lauren's heart, and she studied him as he carried Joe through to his bedroom.

Was he all right, Jean-Luc? Although she'd seen—and sometimes kissed—the dreadful scars from operations he'd had on his leg, she'd never asked about other injuries he might have had from the typhoon. Or from other accidents in the past ten years. Or from illnesses.

She knew absolutely nothing about the man, yet had

fallen so deeply in love with him that hearing tiredness in his voice made her heart hurt.

Once in Joe's room, she changed her sleepy son into his pyjamas, steered him into the bathroom to use the toilet, then cleaned his teeth and tucked him into bed.

'He won't remember any of this in the morning—the going-to-bed part,' she told Jean-Luc, because talking to him about commonplace things was easier than thinking about him. 'It's happened before that I've had to change him when he's already fallen asleep and he goes straight back to sleep as if he was never disturbed.'

Jean-Luc gave her a glance that seemed to say, OK, let's talk commonplaces.

'He did well, dialling triple O and giving his address. It wasn't his fault they sent a police car rather than an ambulance.'

'I can't take any credit for that,' Lauren said. They were standing in the doorway of Joe's room, looking at him, relaxed and breathing easily in his sleep. 'He was taught that at school. All the kids learn and even the most disabled ones know their names and addresses or have a tag they can show people. It's wonderful to find that the teaching actually works in a real-life situation.'

She turned out the light and moved away and, knowing Jean-Luc was following, added, 'Thank you for coming to his rescue. He must have been terrified, being here on his own in an emergency.'

'He was sensible enough to tell Lucy to get me,' Jean-Luc reminded her, 'and as it turned out, while I'm sorry it took Mrs West being ill, the incident has done me a big favour.'

Lauren was halfway down the passageway and she halted, looking back at him.

'A big favour?'

'Yes,' he replied but said no more, so she continued in the direction of the front door.

Did he want her to ask what it was? Was this a ploy to get her talking to him?

She hovered at the door to the sitting room, looking towards the front door of the flat because she didn't want to look at Jean-Luc.

'May I stay and tell you what it was?'

He was right beside her, paler than ever, and it was all she could do not to lift her hand and cup it around his cheek as she had done so many times before.

'Well, I can hardly kick you out when you've come to the rescue so valiantly this evening, now can I?' Lauren grouched, but though Jean-Luc usually smiled when she was grumpy, he didn't smile this time.

'Not exactly welcoming me with open arms, but it will do,' he said, his voice sounding as strained as his face looked. 'In the kitchen or the living room?'

'The living room,' Lauren said. 'You sound very serious and the kitchen is a casual place.'

He nodded and led the way, taking the chair in which he'd been sitting earlier, holding Joe in his arms.

'I had time, before Russ came home, to do a lot of thinking,' he began, while Lauren, sitting on the couch with her legs tucked under her, tried to pretend this was just a chat.

'And I realised I don't want to be on the outside of Joe's life.'

So this is about Joe, not me, she thought, so uncertain whether to be relieved or pleased that she didn't take in the meaning of the words.

'I don't want to not know who's minding him. He's my son, and though he might not understand how and why, I think he should know that, and he should live with me. I know that's awkward, the way things are between you and I, but he *is* my son and he should be my family as well as yours.'

The words weren't even beginning to make sense. Lauren frowned at him.

'I've no worries about telling him you're his father, but living with you—Jean-Luc, the reason I still live so close to my mother at my age is because someone always has to be here for Joe when he's at home and I'd rather have family minding him than a series of nannies or au pairs. You're at work all day and sometimes half the night—how can you look after a little boy?'

He shook his head.

'I am not explaining myself very well,' he said, then he muttered away in French, not to her, she thought, but to himself. 'What I am saying is that I want us to be a family—you and me and Joe. Your family, of course, will still be part of his life and in time he will know my family as well, but it is the three of us that are the family unit and that is what I want.'

Lauren stared at him.

'Are you talking marriage between you and me?' she demanded.

He shrugged.

'If that is what it takes.'

'Boy, that's romance for you!' Lauren exploded. 'If that's what it takes! What woman could resist such a passionate proposal? And what happened to you not wanting to marry again? Didn't you postpone our love-making so you could make it very clear to me you didn't intend marriage? And don't tell me that was before you knew about Joe, because it wasn't!'

'That was then, before I knew I wanted him—before tonight, when I realised I should have been here for him, not up the road where Lucy had to get me, but here.'

Lauren shook her head.

'You're not making sense,' she told him, and to her surprise he agreed.

'I know, because I can't totally explain it even to myself. But sense or not, it's what I want so you may as well get used to the idea and start thinking about how we can make it work,' he said. 'I'll go now!'

And he did! He stood up and walked out of the room, opened the front door and before Lauren could unwind off the couch, she heard it shut.

Which left her precisely where?

Not trusting the man who'd suddenly decided he wanted to marry her.

Not for love, of course, but for more access to his son!

No, she couldn't think about that—it hurt too much.

And just where was he expecting to live this married life?

Back in France?

That thought excited her. Now she remembered the young Jean-Luc talking of his village, of the deep blue Mediterranean curling around the cliffs at Cassis, she felt a longing to see it and experience a different way of life.

Wouldn't this be better than going to the US to become a perfusionist?

More of a challenge?

And as her mind warmed to the idea her body heated, betraying her by wanting him, although she didn't trust him.

'Don't worry about me in making your decision,' her

mother said when she returned and Lauren told her of Jean-Luc's sudden proposal. 'I'd love nothing more than to spend time in the south of France. The light is supposed to be magic, and the scenery—a whole new world to paint. I could come over each year for a few months, rent a cottage so I'm not in the way, and Russ and Bill would visit, you know that.'

'Mum!' Lauren protested. 'You coming to visit isn't the issue here. What *I'm* worried about is marrying the man.'

'Why? You love him. That's obvious enough. And if you love him, why not marry him?'

Lauren stared at her mother.

'It's not that easy,' she protested. 'He only wants to marry me so he can have Joe—so we can be a family!'

'Are you sure of that?'

'It's what he said.'

'Ah, but men don't always get it right when they say things,' her mother said.

Lauren huffed her ridicule.

'I can hardly mistake "I want us to be a family" for "I love you", now, can I?'

'No?'

'You're impossible!'

Her mother smiled but it was the saddest expression Lauren had ever seen on her mother's face.

'Your father never said "I love you" to me, not once, but it was there in every flower he planted in the garden, every pay cheque he brought home and gave to me, every kiss he gave you and Russ, and every time he took me in his arms.'

Lauren stared at her mother. She'd been too young to remember her father, who had been killed in a car crash, and this was the first time she'd ever heard her mother talk of him that way—talk of love!

'Is love enough?' she asked her mother. 'Even when you've doubts?'

'I think it's enough,' her mother said. 'I'll sleep in your flat in case you decide you want to talk to him.'

Lauren shook her head, her mind once again in such a muddle she didn't know where to start thinking.

She could, of course, ask him.

But tonight? It was after midnight and he'd looked very tired.

He'd look more tired in the morning if he couldn't sleep, wondering whether she'd accept his strange proposal.

She walked outside and looked along the street. There were lights on in the downstairs flat at number twenty-six.

Slowly she made her way along the footpath, her feet barely lifting, her shoulders bowed as if the distance between their houses was a million miles. Up the path to the front door—she lifted her hand, hesitated, wanting to scoot right back home.

Then knocked.

'Lauren!'

Good, he seemed surprised, though she doubted she'd caught him as much off guard as he'd caught her earlier.

'Are you going to ask me in?'

His turn to hesitate, then he opened the door wider and with an expansive gesture waved her in. And as she passed him she caught a whiff of alcohol on his breath, explained when she entered the sitting room and saw the brandy bottle and the balloon glass, dark liquid in the base of it.

'One brandy and that not even finished,' he assured her, as if guessing she might not talk to him if he'd been drinking. 'Do you want one? It's the cognac you liked at the restaurant.'

Before we came home and made love all night.

'No, thank you. I just came to ask you something.'

He waited until she'd curled up on the couch then he sat down and picked up his glass, cradling the rounded shape of it in his hands and slowly swirling the liquid round and round.

Brandy tastes better slightly warm, she remembered him saying at the restaurant, then realised she was allowing herself to be distracted because she really didn't want to ask him what she'd come to ask.

'So, you have a question?' he prompted, and though she tried to read his mood in his face, his eyes, his voice, he seemed to have shut himself off from her.

As she had from him over the past week…

'Do you love me?'

The words blurted from her lips. It had seemed the only way to get them out and now they hung there in the air between them, like sleeping bats—dark and somehow dangerous for all their stillness.

'Of course,' he said, a suggestion of a smile flirting around his lips.

It was the smile that aggravated her the most.

'That's easy to say but why should I believe you?' she demanded.

'Ah!' he said, and took a sip of brandy. 'I believe it's about trust. That's what it's always been about between us, Lauren. Ten years ago you accused me of betraying Therese and, because, to a certain extent, that was true, I couldn't deny it. But Therese and I had been separated for months before I went to India—before, against all the odds, I met a young woman from Australia and fell desperately in love. I told you then—the day we quarrelled—that it was you I loved, and even when I thought you were dead, I still loved you.'

'That doesn't make sense,' Lauren said, wondering if it was her muddled mind or if he really was talking in riddles.

'Let's start with Therese. We married young—too young—both of us just out of school. I was studying and she felt neglected and in the end we separated. She wasn't happy in our marriage but she wasn't happy about that either, and it was one of the reasons I went to India—to put some distance between us so we could both sort things out. Then at St Catherine's I met you and I discovered what love was all about. I fell in love with a gangly, freckled, wonderful young woman who radiated kindness and compassion and love for all who met her. How could I not fall in love?'

Lauren wasn't sure if she was supposed to answer that question but as his words had made a lump form in her throat she couldn't speak so she sat and waited to see where this was going.

'I wrote to Therese straight away. I told her all about you and how much I loved you and said I knew she'd meet someone she could love the same way one day, which was why we should both be free. I was confirming our marriage was over, saying again what I'd said before, but this time, because I loved you, I thought she'd understand. Of course it must have hurt her, and that's why she wrote back—the letter you saw that day—and said it didn't matter because she knew I'd come back to her eventually.'

'And did you?'

He shook his head.

'She wanted that, but although I thought you were dead it still seemed wrong. I would have been cheating Therese if I'd gone back to her—and cheating your memory as well. So we divorced as soon as possible.'

He paused, sighing at his memories.

'Later, thinking parents of young children would feel easier if I were married, I became engaged to Justine but still, in my heart, I felt it was wrong. In the end, she broke off our engagement, blaming my preoccupation with my work. I didn't know it at the time—didn't know it, in fact, until I met you again and suddenly my work, though still extremely important, wasn't the most important thing in my life. But you were right, I had betrayed both of them. Betrayed them because somewhere deep inside me you were still my one true love.'

Lauren let the words sink in. Could this really be? Could he have loved her in his heart all this time?

And if so, why had he made such a production of telling her their love-making wouldn't lead to marriage?

She had to ask, but how?

There was only one way—blurt it out!

'Why marriage now, when you were so insistent earlier there'd be no marriage? Is it because of Joe? Is it just for him you want to marry me now?'

He set the brandy balloon down on the table and came towards her, settling on the couch beside her but not touching her.

'You must understand I had made a…hash of two serious relationships and blamed the failure for both on my work. I had decided if I was made that way—in such a way that work would always come first—then I could not hurt another woman by marrying her then letting her down. It is only in this last week that I've realised there's a work-Lauren ratio. With no Lauren there was something in my subconscious that prompted me to work all the hours possible in order to forget you, but now I've found you again, I don't need to do that. I would not marry you for Joe, although I do want to live with him as my son, but I would marry you because I love you, Lauren. The big question is, do you love me?'

She studied his face, pale, tired and anxious, then finally gave in to the impulse to cradle his cheeks in her hands, and once she held him captive it seemed only natural to kiss him.

'I do love you,' she whispered into the kiss. 'I fell in love with you almost from the start—this time around. It frightened me, because I'd never felt that way before—well, not that I could remember—but I wonder if it was because you were always there, just lost somewhere in my mind that I couldn't get to. Then I remembered the letter and it brought back not only the good memories but the bad ones as well and I began to wonder if I could trust you.'

'And trust—you have trust now?' he asked, easing away from her.

'I do, because that's what love's about after all! Without that as a foundation even the deepest love could falter.'

'So I should be saying I trust you, not I love you, *ma biche*?' Jean-Luc teased—now teasing her with kisses as well as words.

Lauren kissed him back while she thought about it.

'No,' she said, after a long time, 'we have to know the trust is there, as the basis of our love—that's part of trust—so we can stick to "I love you" when we say it, and I do love you, Jean-Luc, though before we get too involved here, I'd like to know what a *"biche"* is. I don't want you calling me "my donkey" or something like that.'

He laughed again, and held her tightly in his arms.

'It means a deer—a little deer—and is an endearment I have only ever used for you—in my mind only, this last week, but now I am able to say it, and will continue to say it.'

'My little deer—I like that—partly, I suppose, because it's like our English dear, spelt d-e-a-r.'

He stopped her with another kiss.

'Are we to translate our languages to each other all night or should we instead communicate in ways that need no words?'

Lauren gave him her answer without words....

CHAPTER ELEVEN

THEY had the big world atlas open on the kitchen table, Joe poring over it. He already knew where France was—or at least could pick out the coloured shape that was the country which was to be his home. He even knew Marseilles was down the bottom and by sliding his chubby finger towards the centre of the page he could come to Cassis.

'Here!' he said, showing Lauren for perhaps the thousandth time. 'This is where we're going to live. And Lucy, too. She will have to learn to bark in French so other dogs will understand her. I know French. I know *bonjour.*'

Lauren heard the flat door open and, knowing it was Jean-Luc, went to greet him, giving him a kiss then leaning against him in the doorway, as Joe practised his *bonjour* on Lucy. She and Jean-Luc both smiled at the strangled pronunciation, but Joe was right—he did already know some French words, Jean-Luc having proved a very patient teacher and Joe a far more adept learner than Lauren herself.

Although she blamed her lack of improvement on the fact that Jean-Luc *was* her teacher, and just being near him made her think of things far removed from French lessons.

'He seems happy enough about going to live in France, but the father thing?' Jean-Luc asked, and Lauren, knowing how anxious Jean-Luc was about being accepted as Joe's father, gave him a quick hug.

'Wait here,' she said, and disappeared into Joe's room, returning with his school workbook. She handed it to Joe.

'Do you want to show us the picture you drew at school today?' she said, and Joe eagerly opened up the book, leafing through the pages. And there, towards the back, he found his drawing.

'Who's in the picture, Joe?' Lauren prompted.

Joe held it up.

'My family,' he said proudly. 'This is my dad—that's you, John—and Mum, and me, and that's Lucy near my feet.'

Lauren felt Jean-Luc stiffen then he stepped forward and picked up the book, staring down at the picture his son had drawn. 'My Family', it said at the top and if the 'a' was backwards, that was of no account. No, what held his attention, what had his finger rubbing gently over the page, was the three-letter word beneath the stick drawing of a man.

'Dad!' he whispered, the word strangled on its way out by the lump in his throat. 'Is that OK with you, Joe? Having me for a dad?'

Joe left his chair and came to stand beside his father. He put his arms around Jean-Luc's waist and hugged him.

'It's what I wished, blowing out my candles,' he said simply. 'For you to be my dad. But I couldn't tell or the wish wouldn't come true.'

Lauren saw the joy in her son's face and the tears in her lover's eyes, and the emotion of the moment was so overwhelming there was nothing she could do but hug them both.

Her family!

4 FREE

BOOKS AND A SURPRISE GIFT!

We would like to take this opportunity to thank you for reading this Mills & Boon® book by offering you the chance to take FOUR more specially selected titles from the Medical™ series absolutely FREE! We're also making this offer to introduce you to the benefits of the Mills & Boon® Book Club™—

- ★ FREE home delivery
- ★ FREE gifts and competitions
- ★ FREE monthly Newsletter
- ★ Exclusive Mills & Boon Book Club offers
- ★ Books available before they're in the shops

Accepting these FREE books and gift places you under no obligation to buy, you may cancel at any time, even after receiving your free shipment. Simply complete your details below and return the entire page to the address below. You don't even need a stamp!

YES! Please send me 4 free Medical books and a surprise gift. I understand that unless you hear from me, I will receive 6 superb new titles every month for just £2.99 each, postage and packing free. I am under no obligation to purchase any books and may cancel my subscription at any time. The free books and gift will be mine to keep in any case.

M9ZED

Ms/Mrs/Miss/Mr ....Initials ....
BLOCK CAPITALS PLEASE

Surname ....

Address ....

....

....Postcode..

Send this whole page to:
UK: FREEPOST CN81, Croydon, CR9 3WZ